GW00983470

# Mr HORNUNG'S THREE GODDESSES

*Hornung-related books produced by Peter Rowland:*

*as biographer:*
RAFFLES AND HIS CREATOR:
THE LIFE AND WORKS OF E.W.HORNUNG (1999)

*as editor:*
HIS BROTHER'S BLOOD (2015)
THE GRAVEN IMAGE (2016)

*as compiler:*
TALL TALES AND SHORT 'UNS (2015)
STINGAREE RIDES AGAIN (2016)


*The works of E.W.Hornung:*

## Stories
UNDER TWO SKIES (1892)
SOME PERSONS UNKNOWN (1898)
THE AMATEUR CRACKSMAN (1899)
THE BLACK MASK (1901)
A THIEF IN THE NIGHT (1905)
STINGAREE (1905)
WITCHING HILL (1913)
THE CRIME DOCTOR (1914)
OLD OFFENDERS AND A FEW OLD SCORES (1923) *(published posthumously)*

## Novels
A BRIDE ROM THE BUSH (1890)
TINY LUTTRELL (1893)
THE BOSS OF TAROOMBA (1894)
THE UNBIDDEN GUEST (1894)
THE ROGUE'S MARCH (1896)
MY LORD DUKE (1896)
YOUNG BLOOD (1898)
DEAD MEN TELL NO TALES (1899)
THE BELLE OF TOORAK (1900)
PECCAVI (1900)
THE SHADOW OF THE ROPE (1902)
AT LARGE (1902)
NO HERO (1903)
DENIS DENT (1903)
MR JUSTICE RAFFLES (1909)
THE CAMERA FIEND (1911)
FATHERS OF MEN (1912)
THE THOUSANDTH WOMAN (1913)

# Mr Hornung's Three Goddesses

## -  a Victorian novelist at work

Peter Rowland

an assessment of the truncated text of
*Goddesses Three* by E.W. Hornung

Nekta Publications

(2017)

ISBN: 978-1-326-89733-8

# Prelims

There are two notes and one very long manuscript. With due obeisance to *Howard's End*, one might as well begin with the notes. The first is on a scrap of paper approximately four inches square. In relatively large script, it is headed 'Chapter I' and runs as follows:

> Here at all events she will live strictly & quietly. English home life. Opportunities to think & to reflect, or to profit by example; and no friction, I hope no frivolities to distract. It is a responsibility for us all. Lead her in the right way.

Boxed into the bottom right-hand corner, in extremely small script, are the supplementary words:

> later, to daughter - - "Don't encourage her to talk about Lisbon; let her forget it; from the few words she let drop — from all I' —

There follows, in theory, "could gather" or "could glean", but the scrap of paper has now ended.

The second note is on a strip of paper measuring exactly 2½ by 8 inches. It lists three precise points which the author is reminding himself to make about a particular character:

> Is spending the long at Cambridge, reading: home for day or two. Will go back *before* breakfast.

> Further reference to hussy-gazing.

> He had played the rather commonplace part of wild undergrad.

1

At which point, after assimilating what are (from our point of view) fundamentally "trailers", we must turn to the actual manuscript. It consists of eleven chapters and the opening paragraph of a twelfth.

The first page is, seemingly, a mess. Measuring 6½ by 8 inches, but in much more fragile condition than the one hundred and ninety-one which follow, it has been written on in black pencil and appears, at first glance, largely indecipherable. There is, admittedly, a title at the head of it, slightly to the right of centre, consisting of two words — *Goddesses Three*. Each of these words has been emphatically underlined three times over. But before one can reach that title, and written diagonally on the left side of the page in almost equally large script, are the words "*Está minto tarde.*"

Beneath these two inscriptions, in much smaller writing (and also underlined three times) is the sub-title "Chapter I". And then come, with several crossings-out and inter-ballooning of fragments, two paragraphs (seemingly) of text which run, in all, to nineteen lines. By this time, just as one's eyes become acclimatised to the contents of a darkened room after some initial shock and bewilderment, so it is possible to actually *read* the words.

The first paragraph consists of no more than one sentence, which runs as follows:

> A girl of 17 stood at an open window overlooking Trafalgar Square, apparently lost in contemplation of that celebrated site: within the room, which was a private one of moderate elegance, a gentleman of 50 sat in an easy chair.

But this was a false start. Rather than seizing a clean sheet of paper and beginning all over again, the novelist struck a line through those words and re-commenced his story immediately underneath them. This time he will keep going.

2

It is hoped, indeed, that the reader will also keep going, for as far at any rate as E.W. Hornung himself was able to travel at some point in the mid-1890s, and that we will meet again, for explanations, assessment and conclusions, at the end of the journey. The novelty of this particular unfinished book is that (unlike *The Graven Image* and *His Brother's Blood*) it is very much a work in progress, with internal jottings and queries, and that it is possible to look over the novelist's shoulder and gain some inkling into how he went about his task — and for us too to be "lost in contemplation" of a celebrated author determinedly at work, very much in a world of his own creation.

Or was it?

# Goddesses Three

## [ by E.W. HORNUNG ]

## Chapter I: *Untitled*

In an elegant apartment overlooking Trafalgar Square, a
gentleman of fifty was gazing at a girl of seventeen, whose
back was turned to him. They were father and daughter,
though one would scarcely have guessed it — save the hotel
official who had registered them on their arrival as Mr James
and Miss Camilla Pontifex. For James was a short, light-haired,
light-eyed Englishman — a most ordinary gentleman indeed;
and Camilla was his uncompromising opposite in all these
respects, resembling him, indeed, only in her height. Miss
Pontifex added great height to his other cubic dimensions;
Camilla was decidedly tall for a girl; but just as decidedly was
her figure slim, her hair and eyes equally dark, and her
complexion — by comparison — free from colour. At the
moment, indeed, there was colour in as much of her face as
her fond father was permitted to behold, and her ear was
nothing less than red-hot; but this was due to the August sun,
which was dipping into the sea of slates across the Square.

4

The time, in fact, was thirty-five minutes past six o'clock by Mr Pontifex's watch, for which, it must be admitted, that gentleman's eyes frequently forsook the charming figure at the window. He was in fact awaiting an arrival; but his daughter, who was watching for it, was the first to express their common impatience. And she expressed it in a foreign tongue:

"*Está minto tarde*," said the girl at last.

"Yes, he *is* late," answered her father; "but look here, Camilla, you must try to speak English. We are not in Lisbon now, we're in England, and your uncle will be here any minute."

"It is true; but I am so stupid!"

"Not a bit; you can speak English as well as I can when you aren't nervous; and there's immediate occasion for your very best English now."

"Very well, I try," said Camilla, who perhaps felt, for her part, that there was occasion for nervousness too.

"I don't want him to find my little girl more than one half Portuguese," added Mr Pontifex.

"At the same time I have lived in Portugal all my life and in Leesbon."

She had been born there, too; whatever her English father might say, no impartial person would have agreed with him that Camilla was only one half Portuguese. His wishes fathered the opposite thought. When a very young man, the lines of James Pontifex had fallen in foreign waters; for twenty years, and indeed down to the last four or five, he had found too many good fish in those seas to tempt him to others; but though he had amassed an agreeable amount of money in Portugal, his feeling towards the Portuguese race was, one fears, somewhat regrettably Britannic in character. He still

5

regarded them with a kind of affectionate contempt which must have been particularly galling had it not been the one sentiment which he troubled himself to conceal. The good man, in short, was tenaciously British at heart, if less so on the surface than he imagined. The only pure Portuguese whom he had ever been able to admire was his wife; and she had died a mere girl, but little older than Camilla was now.

Now Camilla, who resembled her father so little, was the speaking image of her mother. Nor did the likeness, as it increased with years, grow into the old wound; Mr Pontifex was a cheerful person; he would not speak of his wife without wincing, and look again into her sweet foreign face, in their daughter, without much gravity in his own. But that he idolised the child as he had idolised her mother was plain in their lightest relations. It was specially plain as he gazed at her now; and on this occasion it must be owned that his gaze was not free from sadness; but the reason for this was itself something special. Yet the present moment ultimately ended in an abrupt uprising of the father and a rather heavy hand on Camilla's shoulder.

"We'll watch for your uncle together, *menina*," he whispered; and proceeded to watch for him in Camilla's sunlit hair.

"*Menina!*" laughed the girl. "Who speaks Portuguese now?"

"One word doesn't count," he answered, with an elephantine story (and this was one respect in which he was less the incurable Briton than he believed himself to be).

"All right — Senhor."

"Don't say 'all right' too often, *menina*; it's all right now and again — "

He stopped to join the laugh against himself which Camilla

was quick enough to raise.  The moment after she was exclaiming against the unknown uncle for his unpunctuality; it would make them so late for dinner ("deener", she called it); and they had not yet "secured seats".

"Your uncle may not care about the theatre," observed Mr Pontifex.

"Ah! He is a padre!"

"You will make his hair stand on end if you tell him so.  He's a clergyman — 'clergyman' is the word, Camilla — and I rather expect he's the kind of clergyman who would greatly object to being called padre. But it is really time he was here. Have you seen nothing in the shape of a padre — as you are *not* to call him."

Camilla replied confidently: "Nothing!"

Nor had she, to her knowledge, seen anything in the shape of the unknown Uncle Anthony; but her knowledge was both limited and antiquated, being derived solely from photographs in an obsolete style.  She did not realise that her uncle Anthony was now, as he had been when that photograph had been taken, many years older than her father, being indeed his step-brother only.  Thus a white-haired, hook-nosed old gentleman, who wore neither clerical collar nor a clerical hat, had been allowed to alight from his four-wheeler and enter the hotel without attracting any of Camilla's suspicions, though these were alert.  Yet this gentleman had given down below the name of Pontifex, which had commanded its own respect, as identical with that of the proprietor of private rooms. A certain servility of respect developed, among the splendid officials, towards the tall old gentleman, though he did insist on carrying his own bag; even as James Pontifex jumped up from his chair, Anthony was in process of considering the room, frowning at the general magnificence.

7

Thus the arrival which Camilla had desired to break came in the end with startling suddenness. As the door opened her arm slid instinctively within her father's, but it slipped as her father darted forward and seized his brother's disengaged hand with both his own.

Camilla watched the meeting with a beating heart and but little presence of mind. That night in the darkness she recollected that most of the cordiality, and all the smiles, had been on her father's side; and she lay awake wondering why Uncle Anthony looked so uniformly stern, and — and how he tied his necktie. The latter was thick, and, like many other points about this clergyman, an anachronism, being in fact neither more nor less than an old-fashioned choker. Camilla had never seen such a thing before; and it was no wonder that she was perplexed.

But these things did not strike her at the time; they were photographs taken then but developed later. At the time Camilla looked on and trembled, she did not exactly know why; and when told in Portuguese to shake hands with her uncle — she required to be told — her response was perhaps the least grateful performance of her life. It was certainly not in her best manner. Something in the old gentleman's eye, which was a steely blue, disconcerted her entirely; it was as if she felt his shadow across her life before he himself had entered into it. Indeed, the expression with which he regarded her delicate beauty was almost as stony as that provoked by the room. She coloured in patches, like rose-leaves, on either side; and on the whole her deportment at this moment was certainly not better than that of an English schoolgirl, and anything but a fair sample of Camilla. Immensely to her relief her father presently hinted to her, in unpremeditated Portuguese, that she might as well go down to the reading room; and she went.

The clergyman, refusing an easy chair, sat down on one that made James Pontifex himself so uncomfortable, that the latter planted himself on the hearthrug with his hands in his pockets.

"What has become of your daughter, James?" said Anthony presently; which left James little more at his ease than the girl had been.

"She has gone down to the reading-room."

"What, alone?"

"Yes; is that seldom done in this country?" inquired James, pleasantly. "She's all right, bless you; she knows many of the establishment by now."

"But why send her out at all?" inquired Anthony, suspiciously.

The embarrassment of James became conspicuous. "Because it was in order to talk to you about her that you've been so good — I meant to say, that I begged you run up to town to see; I take it very kindly of you, Anthony, to have come."

"I did not come without considerable inconvenience," said the clergyman, ungraciously; "I seldom leave Essingham and at my time of life even a three hour railway journey is an undertaking."

"An undertaking? It must be; and you are hot and tired, I see you are; for which reason, and also because we have not seen each other since we were young men," added cheerful Mr James, not very felicitously, as he moved towards the bell, "I shall ring for the waiter and order — "

"Nothing to drink, I hope: because I never drink anything."

James shrugged his shoulders good naturedly; but he was not yet at ease; for his brother's manner was not reassuring.

His tone was uncomfortably brusque; and as James looked down at the cold eyes, set slightly too close together, with aquiline nose and the closely-shut mouth, the thought occurred to him neither to say what he had meant to say and not to do what he had resolved to do. But [as] for this reason he had sent for his brother; the reason at least must come out, and, after all, if Anthony's features were too much the stern brother as he remembered him twenty years ago, his hair and whiskers, black then, were now white as snow; and there is that which inspires confidence in very black hair. And the view he was [now] disposed to take of his brother [would be a fresh view]. As he hesitated, Anthony remarked cheerfully —

"So it is only to show me your daughter that you have sent for me all this way — and to talk about her. Why didn't you bring her to see me?"

"Well, that did seem the natural thing to do; but the fact is I am here on the most urgent business, and all my time is taken up. I was in the City at ten this morning; I should be there still if it had not been for your coming; and I shall be there at ten o'clock tomorrow, and every day for a week or two. Then I may have to rush up to Glasgow, or Liverpool, then back to Lisbon; and then —   The fact is, Anthony, we are forming in Lisbon a company for the planting of sugar in Mozambique, where we have obtained a concession at particularly advantageous terms; and I, a managing director, am over here publicising the project."

"I hope you do not want me to take any shares in your company," remarked Anthony.

"The shares are already all taken by private individuals in Lisbon," James had the satisfaction of informing him. "No, I have told you why I begged you to come — and very good I think you to have done so; it was to talk to you about my daughter."

"Now I am here, then, what about her?"

"The difficulty is, where to begin," said James, with some embarrassment; "we have corresponded so seldom, and it is next to impossible to give you a proper impression of my surroundings out there. However, for the last twelve years, since my wife's death, Camilla and I have lived with her people. I daresay I mentioned to you, at the time of my marriage, that they were rather distinguished folks, in their way; however my father-in-law, who is a gay young man of seventy, is a Count, one of the Portuguese nobility, and as poor as a rat. However, some years ago the Government made him a present, one of the forts of the Tagus, where he spends most of his time, and where Camilla has been brought up under my eye. She has had as good an education as the country could give her; she can speak fluently three languages; she reads English books; and her singing, I think, will please you. In fact the management has answered uncommonly well until now; but now that she is grown up I don't think it answers quite so well; for — you understand me, Anthony — our ways in Lisbon are not the English ways, by any means!"

Anthony could quite understand that.

"And I have got to hanker after the English ways — for Camilla. Not that they are not a kind-hearted people; only they're such hopeless foreigners! Nor would I wish to uproot Camilla from what is, after all, her native land, if I could always be with her there. But the fact is, I shall have to go out to Mozambique for at least a year to set the Company going — the Portuguese would wreck it in a month! What Englishman wouldn't be so employed who hasn't been abroad?"

11

Anthony had been nodding his head but now leaned back and ceased to nod.

"That climate would kill Camilla; besides our concession is a hundred miles on the Zambezi. But can I let her turn into an out-and-out Portuguese in my absence?"

Still the clergyman sat rigid.

"Anthony," cried James in desperation, "you must see what I mean! You have two girls of your own, about Camilla's age, you live in the house where we were both born — and you must enter into my feelings, for like me, you have lost your wife. The truth is, I want you to take care of my little girl for me while I am away."

At last he got an answer.

"I guessed as much from your letter. I suppose I ought to take your hand and say it is settled! I am not taken by surprise: this crossed my mind in the train, but — you must excuse me, James, it requires consideration."

"Of course it does — if you will only consider it!" cried James, thankfully, the cloud of a dreaded instant refusal removed from his heart.

"The Spanish religion is, if I mistake not, Roman Catholic."

"The Portuguese religion? To be sure, it is."

"Then your wife was a Roman Catholic."

James nodded — rather haughtily, for him. "She was," he said, shortly.

"But your daughter — your daughter is a Protestant, naturally."

"No, I am sorry to say she is not; my boy would have been a Protestant, had he lived; but Camilla inherits her mother's religion — that was the condition under which I married. Does it make a difference?"

"I am surprised that you submitted to a condition so

12

iniquitous, for of course it does make a difference," said Anthony, with a severity that would have been more becoming thirty years earlier. "May I ask if you yourself have since gone over to the Church of Rome?"

James was keeping his temper with success, though not without difficulty: there were things in his recollection, when Anthony was a clergyman of forty and he himself a young fellow in the twenties, which had prepared him for a more disagreeable reception of his proposal than he had met with. He was encouraged, rather than otherwise. Anthony was a good man, whatever else he might be: and he would soon love Camilla for her own sake as all the world did. As for religion, it was not a strong point with James, but his sympathies, such as they were, were with the Church of which he was himself a member. So he answered with perfect good humour:

"No; I haven't turned papist. You haven't much time to keep up your religion in a business life; but I will come to hear you preach, Anthony, in the dear old church, if I have time before I sail; and if you were to convert Camilla I wouldn't personally make a row about it — only I don't think you will succeed in doing so."

The clergyman frowned, perhaps only naturally. Yet apparently the situation presented itself to him in a kindlier light than at first. At any rate he rose for the first time from his chair, went to the window, and stood here for some minutes, looking out in silence.

The sun had set, at least on Trafalgar Square, and the opposite buildings clipped a sky of ripe red, softened by the impalpable London haze, as often the colour of a plum is softened by the bloom: the fountains reared snow-white mists against the creeping shadows; the Admiral and his coil of rope were drawn in ink on paper of a more delicate tint than the wit of stationer has yet devised. The well-known scene was not exactly familiar to Anthony Pontifex, because he seldom came to town, and when he did this was not the quarter in which he stayed. The sight and sound of the traffic was as strange to him as it was to Camilla; for Lisbon is at all events a city but Essingham is a village of three hundred souls all told. He would not have said that it was strange at all; but it impressed him; and it was with a comparative remark touching London and the country — and he did not seem to have been thinking of anything else — that he presently turned from the window.

"Yes, this is about the most stagnant [time] — the second half of August — of the whole stagnant season," answered James; "there is simply nothing on."

"Nothing of what?"

"Theatres, for example: or very little in the way of what we thought of going to see tonight: I suppose you wouldn't care about it?"

"If there is one place I would *not* set foot in, on any consideration whatever, it is a theatre; and I am surprised that you should think of taking your daughter to one."

"We won't go; I am tired as it is; Camilla won't mind."

"She may mind, but she certainly won't go, while she is in *my* charge," said Anthony, involuntarily betraying the bent of his ruminations at the window.

"Then you *will* take charge of her?" cried James, delightedly.

"I will consider it."

And he did. He considered it acutely when Camilla appeared charmingly dressed for dinner (for which the gentlemen did not dress); and still more acutely when he had counted the glasses of wine Camilla drank at the glittering table d'hôte, when they dined, in preference to privacy, at Camilla's coyest petition. The wine did not get into her head; so much the more shame for a girl of eighteen. The clergyman considered it very sincerely indeed, over his cold water, and with the most entire sincerity. Clearly she was a pitiable case. Religion apart, the girl was on the brink of a precipice from which it would be but Christian to save even a Roman Catholic. Certainly it was something new to the Reverend Anthony Pontifex to hold out a helping hand to any one beyond the pale of his own Church; but this pervert was James's child; and he had leave to convert her, if he could. "I can; and I will," said he, but to himself; aloud he said — "You must give me until the morning; and if she is come at all, she had better go back with me tomorrow, and see how she likes it."

He had, however, already decided in his own mind: and Camilla's fate was settled. He did not give her another thought after retiring to the room his half-brother and host had engaged for him. His thoughts took an eccentric turn before getting into bed. His last act was to put his boots out: a pair of boots on almost every mat in the corridor soon attracted his attention; and it occurred to him that from the man who cleaned them, *his* boots would obtain not an atom more of attention than these twenty-nine other pairs. Now at Essingham the personality of the Rector, and all that appertained to it, was nothing less than sacred; and Mr Pontifex would have liked to be shown the parishioner who would not black his boots, and black them with the most particular pains. He suffered a twinge of homesickness; he ascribed it to the strange bed, but it was this thought, which occupied a dark corner of his venerable skull, where it could not be inspected, until sleep timed it out.

15

And while the Reverend Anthony Pontifex lay troubled by a sense of shrunken individuality (requiring a pretence that it was merely the strange bed); and while Camilla sleepily wondered why that gentleman so seldom smiled, and how in the wide world he fastened his cravat; her poor father smoked a pipe in his pyjamas, because he could not sleep for thinking. "If I lose her at all it is tomorrow. Tomorrow night my little girl will be gone!" His habitual cheerfulness had for once deserted him.

# Chapter II: *Untitled*

The following morning at 10.55 an ordinary Inland Telegram was handed in at the Charing Cross office, which cost the sender five shillings, although the entire message was contained in eleven words.  At 11.19 it was received at Hillston and handed by the postmaster to his son, who, in a commendably short space of time, was clattering across the market-place on horseback, with the telegram in his pocket.  It was the very morning for a country canter: a glowing sun, a cloudless sky, and really a delightful breeze, when one rode to meet it.  On such a morning the "well-built market-town" (as you may find Hillston truly ticketed, in the *History, Gazetteer and Directory* of the County) would generate an uncomfortable degree of dry heat, by reason of its many stones; and the postmaster's son turned his back on it with the joy that was all the keener for coming in the way of business.  He did not draw rein until he reached the cross-roads where the sign-post stood in its triangle of grass; but he did not look at the sign-post; the way to Essingham he knew blindfold; the great thing was, that, for the whole four miles from this, there was neither turn, nor house, nor fence nor hedge on either hand.  In fact, this road crosses one of the open spaces of England, where you shall see no grass certainly, but pine-trees at all distances, miles of sandy warren to right and left and more rabbits to the square-yard than you ever beheld before, out of a hutch.

It was excusable, or nearly so, in our special messenger, to walk his pony in the shadow of the first plantation, which edged the road.  Later, also, when the pines had receded, and he dismounted to fill his pocket with stones, with intentions towards the teeming rabbits, one could forgive the wilful delay; though Mr Pontifex, J.P. would have taken a less lenient view of the cause, potential poaching, from the Hillston bench. As he himself was the sender of the telegram, delayed in transit by this potential poaching, there is no guessing at the "copy" he would have furnished to the natural enemies of the impar'd buck. It would not have been his first appearance as a radical priest. But Mr Pontifex was in London; even the poacher knew that, and fired shot after shot with a satisfying sense of immunity, and impairing intent, let us add, [towards] the population of that warren. However, it was twenty minutes past twelve before he struck the trees again and turned into Essingham; and that was disgraceful. What must lower him still more in our eyes, was the manner in which he now pulled round and the deceitful pace which he now put on, actually galloping from the old church at the west end of the village to the still older one at its eastern extremity adjoining the Rectory. The clattering hoofs brought forth infirm peasants, the village fathers, at every door: an ostentatious rattle at the Rectory gate produced Miss Winnie Pontifex from the flower-bed flanking the drive, in dirty old dog-skin gauntlets, with a trowel in one hand.

"Telegram, miss!" cried the good youth, reining up in a model hurry.

"Ah, from the Rector," said Winnie, in a calm way which was quite her own.

She slipped off one of the gauntlets, and held up a strong, shapely, pretty hand, but not a small one, for the envelope. This was addressed to "Miss Pontifex" (the Rector wouldn't have omitted the prefix of a Pontifex if he had been cabling from New Zealand), and Winnie, after instinctively gliding a finger under the flap, reflected that she was not Miss Pontifex, and withdrew it.

"You had better go round to the kitchen; there might be an answer; and get them to give you a glass of beer, for I am sure you have ridden very hard!"

"Thank you, miss! Oh, no miss!" said our friend, with infamous modesty; and he went.

Winnie proceeded to the house. It was a long two-storied building, shadowed by elms, with stuccoed walls, jalousied windows, a steep tiled roof, and narrow hall running through the midst of it, which was chiefly remarkable for a miniature bagatelle-table reposing there. Here Winnie stood and called in a loud good-natured voice:

"Constance! Where are you?"

"Here," said Constance, appearing unexpectedly from the stairs, "I do wish you wouldn't call about the house like that, when you know how the Rector hates it."

"The Rector is in London," said Winnie mildly; "here is a telegram from him; it's addressed to you, so I thought I'd better not open it."

"Then how do you know it's from him? Of course you should have opened it," said Constance, opening it herself; but Winnie entertained a satisfying conviction that she had done the right thing. She even watched Constance read it without looking over her shoulder; knowing her sister of old.

The elder girl's forehead became corrugated as she said aloud:

"'Shall arrive with Camilla at 7.24 Hillston. Send wagonette.' Now who on earth is Camilla?" asked Constance, who delighted in density on occasion. "Never heard of her!"

"I have," said Winnie, drily; "it's our cousin, of course."

"Ah, the Portuguese; well, I really never heard of her before the other day; and I don't think the Rector mentioned her name even then, because I don't think he knew it. Camilla!"

"I like it," affirmed Winnie; "and I'm glad she's coming."

"Of course you are; you haven't got the trouble of getting ready for her at a moment's notice. For my part I think it simply outrageous of the Rector to play us a trick like this. But I know what it is; it is not his fault; it's Uncle What's-it!"

"Uncle James," suggested Winnie.

"Uncle James, then — it's Uncle James that's palmed off his daughter upon us! He's failed, I shouldn't be surprised, and lost all his money, and now he wants the Rector to support his child! We shall have this Camilla thing on our hands for the rest of our natural lives; you mark my words!"

Winnie knew better than to do more than mark them. "Well, we must make the best of it," she observed. "Which room shall you give her?"

"Which indeed!" exclaimed Constance. "We don't even know what she is like to look at," she added, inconsequently.

"I say pretty."

Constance did not say ugly; but she looked the word. The word only, however: for Constance was the pretty girl of these two who, as they spoke, faced one another across the tiny bagatelle-table in the shadows of the hall. She had the hereditary blue eyes; her hair was fair, very plentiful, somewhat severely arranged; her nose was perfectly straight, though small, with perfect nostrils; and this more than any other feature stamped her face with character. As for her figure it was small, neat, active, and compact, but an accurate photograph of her face would have convinced you that no other pedestal was possible. The form of Winnie was sadly different: it was of the unlimited order, which may end in corpulence. She was, indeed, already twenty, and had done growing — one way. But one had only to look in her wholesome face to see that long life, and awful possibilities, were before her. Big all over, her wrists and muscles were as those of a man; and her features suffered from a certain lack of refinement. Two outward merits she possessed: her eyes and her hair, which were brown, and the colour in her skin. Herein, and only here, she resembled, as we happen to know, the "Camilla thing": but the English shades were lighter, and more varied in the influence of night shadows. On the whole, however, Winnie Pontifex unconsciously suggested that her father had married slightly beneath him. And this was actually the case, at least from the Rector's own point of view; few families, in his eyes, could supply an absolutely fitting mate for a Pontifex; and as he had married late in life, yet in the end very hurriedly, his choice had been restricted. Even then he had married neither for love nor for money; he had married out of consideration for the family living and its accompanying acres; and was, or perhaps he deserved to be, bitterly disappointed in his only son. However this young gentleman was not in the hall when the disturbing telegram arrived from Charing Cross; as usual, no one had any notion of his whereabouts, though nominally he was at home; and of his sisters no more need be said, save that Constance had a character of many sides, of which the worst was eternally presented to Winnie, who herself was not credited with any character at all.

Thus, at the present juncture, Constance, though all day (with one interval) her tongue took pieces out of the girl she had never seen, and out of the maid who assisted her in preparing the visitor's room, yet had a very charming room ready before evening, and a very excellent supper arranged for: while Winnie, whose tongue was as soft as her eyes, said no unkind thing to or of anyone, put on her old gauntlets and went back to her flower bed, being helped merely by a good-natured dismissal of the post-master's son. Possibly she knew better than to proffer her assistance in any department saved to Constance; certainly experience was her guide whenever Constance was concerned. But Constance, it has been said, had an interval that day in which she neither fumed nor nagged, in which the expression of her face subtly changed, no less than that of her voice; in which, in fact, she was unaffectedly pleasant and amiable. This was during the call of a neighbouring rector, a youngish man, who, in spite of his High Church proclivities had somehow gained the friendship of Mr Pontifex, chiefly, one fancies, by playing bagatelle with him on the tiny table; for this trivial game was a strong man's weakness. Constance was at her best during this call, and her best was not free from sweetness and charm. But when the clergyman was gone her character revolved, and another side showed itself — the satyrical one. She had this odious but entertaining talent to no slight extent: and, oddly enough, the High Church rector (behind his back) was her favourite butt. The High Church was not popular at Essingham, so Constance's treatment of the subject was, rather. As long as she would sit in the house (which was never for very long at a time) Winnie listened to the latest ritualistic touches added to his services by the late visitor, who was an Irishman with many frank and delightful traits; nor could she listen without laughing; but she went out rather vexed with the Irishman for this absurd manner in which he habitually gave himself away, and with Constance as habitually taking advantage of him afterwards, but never at the time him, in her own peculiar fashion. To her mind there was in this something almost dishonourable; but Winnie was not only a little rough externally, but unsophisticated in soul, in comparison with Constance.

It was just eight o'clock, and a starry evening, when the wagonette ground the gravel of the drive, the Rector driving and Camilla at his side, with her luggage and Prentiss (the meek coachman) on the seats behind. The girls met them on the steps, Constance receiving Camilla in a rather demonstrative embrace as she jumped from the wheel. Nor did she cease here to make amends for some of the things she had been saying during the day; for Constance, after all, was hostess, and she enjoyed playing the part. It was she who carried Camilla off to her room, and made friends with her before Winnie had been able to do more than kiss her cheek; and it was Constance, of course, who presently did the honours of the high-tea which she herself had very successfully prepared. The meal, however, was a little dismal. The Rector, for his part, seldom spoke at the table, except to demand a cruet or to storm at the butler (a timid man named Trull) for the crimes of the cook. Tonight he was particularly silent and hungry, but thanks to Constance's personal supervision and preliminary activity, no excuse for present complaint. Constance, whose effort to be delightful was palpable, asked a series of questions about Spain (meaning Portugal) which Camilla did her best to answer. Winnie had few opportunities of joining in the conversation, and it did not strike [her] that she would add to the newcomer's by making use of such as presented themselves. Camilla, indeed, was palpably nervous and tired, and most probably miserable as well; her eyes were very bright and timid, and the signs of suppressed excitement were plain in her cheeks; and it was not until supper was over that Winnie addressed a remark to her, and when she did, it was merely to ask whether she would not like to go to bed. Camilla answered that she would, with a sweet shy smile of gratitude; and merely over this simple question, and its simpler answer, a little exchange of hearts took place then and there.

Ten o'clock, which was soon reached tonight, was the hour for evening prayers at the Rectory. This function, which took place in the drawing-room, was severe rather than solemn (though certainly no one would have ventured to smile). The voice of the Rector, though stern at all times, was never really terrible save in the reading of Holy Writ. Even in his sermon, in those passages which were most open to criticism, it would vibrate with a passion which, if not exalting, was at least human; but in the daily lessons it was merely forbidding, and such as to provoke the profoundest pity for children and servants to whom the Word came in so harsh a tone. Both were forced to hear it. The room was furnished in a style of which the only merit was its comparative antiquity. For prayers the chairs were arranged in set places, so that Mr Pontifex could count absentees at a glance. Tonight there were three: the butler, the coachman (for maidservants and menservants were alike required to attend), and, as was only too commonly the case, the Rector's son, whose movements were regrettably mysterious.

"Where are Trull and Prentiss?" asked Mr Pontifex, in his sternest tones, across the open Bible.

The cook (on whom the master's frown rested) could not say, she was sure. The Rector turned to Constance:

"Where is Anthony?"

"I have no idea; we have not seen him all day."

The Rector's frown deepened visibly; and he read the Bible without relaxing it. Then they knelt down. When they rose from their knees, and the servants filed out, the two girls were requested to retain their chairs, and, resuming his, Mr Pontifex addressed them.

"I have," he said, "an unpleasant thing to tell you respecting your cousin Camilla. She has come here for only a few days certain, but the chances are she will stay for at least this twelvemonth; however, this is not it. Your uncle, who is about to spend a year in Africa, so far as I can see to increase his already sufficient means — an enterprise of which I strongly disapprove — has described to me his life and Camilla's in Lisbon. It has not been the kind of life with which I should like you to be familiar, even by hearsay; and I will have to ask Camilla no questions about it, and never encourage her to speak of it. It has been a life with very little religion in it, and such as there was has not been religion at all, but gross idolatry; for I am shamed to tell you, Constance and Winifred, that Camilla is at present a Roman Catholic."

The information duly affected both girls: Winnie opened her soft eyes wide, but Constance could not restrain a little gasp of horror. They gazed at their father as if stunned by such black news.

"I say at present," continued the Rector, "and I say it advisedly; for I would not have received her into my home on any consideration had not your uncle given me full power to lead his child from the ways of error and rank superstition. As it is I am not sure that I am doing right, but at least I am doing what I conceive to be my duty. It is duty, girls, to save a soul from everlasting fire, and that duty — no less — is ours; for you must help me. Thank God the Catholics have not penetrated hereabouts! — their nearest chapel is at Hillston, and I have done my best to destroy their influence even there. However, I cannot physically restrain Camilla from going there, with their priests, candles and tomfoolery, if she wishes to do so; I wish I could, but I have undertaken not to do so. She will never, of course, have horse or wheel of mine for such a

25

purpose; nor, though she is to have money at her disposal — more money than I approve of — will I allow anyone in the village to furnish her with either; but she might walk. Your uncle, however, thinks she will not care to go, and I trust he is right. Apparently she is indifferent, as he is certainly. He is neither one thing nor the other, but his sympathies, such as they are, still lean towards the Protestant religion and doctrines. He would not be sorry to see his child rescued from false doctrine and schism, as he shall see it yet, and will himself, I hope, come in time to a more serious sense of his responsibilities and his danger, his very terrible danger. There is no more to be said on the subject — to you. But you will both kneel with me once before you go."

They agreed, but of the particular petition which Mr Pontifex now offered up not a word must be said, but that at least it was earnest. And it was not without a certain hard dignity that he arose from his knees. Nor was the kiss he gave the girls, on their foreheads, devoid of kindness; [indeed], it was kinder than usual. They climbed the stairs in silence, and heard the Rector pass out into the grounds as they did so. But on the landing Winnie whispered:

"Poor Camilla!"

"Poor indeed!" said Constance, pityingly.

"Yet I think he was rather hard on the Roman Catholics."

"As if you could be too kind to them!" cried Constance, smacking unpleasantly of her father.

They stood for some minutes by the bannisters for each was impressed, in her own way. "I don't know," murmured Winnie, more than once; but as Constance *did* know, and said so, on each occasion, they got no further, and were going to their rooms when one of them suggested that they should peep in to see whether Camilla was comfortable. This was

Winnie. Constance did not think it necessary, but she would not have Winnie go alone, so they went together; and listening without heard nothing. Then they softly opened the door; and there was Camilla, her dark hair spread half over her shoulders, half on the bed, fast asleep upon her knees.

For a moment both girls were silent. Then one remarked, with a silent laugh:

"So she is not even a firm Catholic!"

This was Constance. Winnie had stepped lightly in front of her to hide what she alone had noticed — a tawdry little picture under Camilla's closed eyes. She had been praying to her saint, and Constance, who was for waking her, was on the point of discovering it; but luckily at this moment the sisters were strangely interrupted; they heard the hall door open violently, and the sound of a well-known voice, in passion, startled their ears.

# Chapter III:  A Clergyman's Son

"A nest of gamblers!  On my premises!  And you the ring-leader — *you*, without a word to say for yourself!"

These were the words, uttered in a towering passion, which met Constance's ears as she hurried out on to the landing. Running halfway downstairs, and looking over the bannisters into the hall, a distressing spectacle greeted her. Winnie had stayed behind to wake Camilla; but in view of a scene such as she had witnessed more than once before, in which the Rector's voice could have been heard in the attics, she restrained herself from doing so, and, shutting the door swiftly behind her, sped impulsively to her sister's side.  She was in time to see their burly brother marching in the hall with his hands in his pockets, and an expression of resignation on his smooth fat face; which contrasted strongly with the Rector's, glaring over his shoulder; and was the more remarkable for the fact that the Rector's sinewy fist gripped the collar of his son's tweed coat.

Mr Pontifex instantly caught sight of his daughters on the stairs.

"Ah, you may well look!  You may well have heard of your brother, who has forgotten what it is to get a hold of himself! And has forgotten what it is to associate with his family, but not to be away from us altogether, no one knows where, or else associates with the very men about the place: drinking — gaming with them — winning their very wages out of their pockets!"

"I happened to lose fivepence," answered the young man, mildly.  "I lost fivepence."

"The amount is no matter, sir!" shouted the Rector, with a shake of the hand on the collar.  "The sin is the same in the sight of Almighty God! A den of drunkards and gamblers!"

"Come, draw the line there, father," said his son, turning round and shaking the hand from the collar, though without removing his own from his pockets; "I'm sober enough, whatever I've done!"

"You are *not*, sir: and that's the main reason for your conduct. Go up to your room, sir, and keep away from us altogether if you come home only to disgrace yourself, and force me to discharge servants who have been here since you were born! Let me see you out of my sight!"

The lad obliged, with merely a shrug of his broad shoulders; but as he swung up the stairs, two at a time, past the girls, he muttered a laconic explanation:

"Saddle-room — penny a corner — Trull, Prentiss, me and Jimmy, And a jug of beer between us!"

The Rector watched him disappear, and listened for his step on the uncarpeted stair leading to the upper storey where his room was. His pale, twitching face, in its venerable pane of silver, was pitiable, certainly. "Go to your rooms, girls," he said, in a rather faint voice; and as they went they heard him bolt the front door, and shut himself up in his study. But they were both more concerned about their brother.

"I expect he *was* tipsy," affirmed Constance, confidentially.

"Then that's all *you* know about it!" cried Winnie, for once; and Constance could only retort, rather weakly, that certainly she had not made a study of tipsiness, though Winnie apparently had.

Meanwhile, Anthony Pontifex the younger (whose reprehensible courses were aggravated at every stage by the name he had been fondly allowed to inherit when a stainless baby) was safely immersed in his den under the tiles. He had

29

two rooms up here, whither (this was one blessing) the Rector never penetrated. Possessed, as he certainly was, of considerable good humour, he was nevertheless a good deal put out by the late scene, though it had been easy, under the insane fury of his father, not to show it. He remained good-humoured but was still feeling the hand on his collar. His first action in his little den was that of "sporting his oak", over which he was [today] very much more particular than it was his habit to be, either at home or at College. It was not [usually] meant for intruders, but he was put out, and the fact was, he half feared a visitation from Constance. Now seeing that young Anthony was really a rather wild young man, and that Constance, to say the least of her, was very particular and very easily shocked, he had a very just appreciation of her good points. But he needed nothing more than what he was so vulgar as to describe as her "pi jaws" — meaning, one supposes, the pious sisterly rebukes with which she sometimes favoured [him]. As a rule, it may be said that he bore these inflictions with uncommon good-nature; but tonight would certainly have furnished an exception; and fortunately Constance never came.

Also, there was a more sympathetic companion than Constance already in the den. As young Pontifex lit the candle, a fox terrier (not a bad one, if its ears had been shorter) jumped out of the arm chair; and his master could not then stop to light the pipe for which he was pining, but sat down deliberately to caress the dog. And he proceeded to pour into the small dog's long ear (the white one — one was lemon-coloured) greater rubbish than one would have expected from a wild young man towards a mere dog. It was a poor beggar, and had it been long there all alone and how had it behaved itself all day? Probably better than its master (the latter confessed), but however that might be, his master would be hanged (and something worse) if he treated him as *he* was treated. And so on in a strain beneath all further comment, addressing the dog by the name of Felix: which sounded absurd until you knew the dog's affectionate disposition and discovered that absurdity suited him. However, even Felix was not a solace for ever. His master presently got up, filled a pipe with birdseye, and began to smoke very furiously, pacing the floor with noiseless feet in the slipshod tennis shoes which he had been wearing all day.

He was a heavy young fellow in point of stature; but there the heaviness ended; his smooth fair face was not only perfectly pleasant, but it had expression, and plenty of it. The expression was chiefly good-humoured, and that to the verge of weakness — perhaps beyond it; also it was lazy, but about the eyes, which were light, there was a look which an observer might have ticketed as one of latent ability. The weakness was in the mouth; on the whole one would have guessed it to be an infirmity of moral purpose rather than of intellect or temper. And that is the worst kind of infirmity, of course; but it is the one kind that is largely due to the bringing-up; and young Pontifex had been brought up very badly indeed — under the lash. His mother had died when he was eight years old — at which age Mr Pontifex had first used the horsewhip to him. To find him at twenty-two, calmly submitting to his father's knuckles between his collar and his neck, is easily to imagine that the horsewhip had continued in use for a considerable number of years. So it had; and Tony's trials were the direct result of the horsewhip. Already he had been once rusticated from Trinity, and some of his goings on in vacation would have closed the Rectory doors on him for ever had the Rector so much as dreamt of them. But Mr Pontifex was becoming hardened to this disappointment and to the product of his unquiet arm; he had given up complaining of unexplained absences, thus flying to extreme laxity from the other extreme; his wrath was kindled only by the sparks that flew in his very eyes. Hence tonight's petty scene. His fault-finding required greater provocation than of old; but a fire of indignation smouldered in the old gentleman's breast; and when really stirred, as tonight, the flame that leapt forth was fiercer than formerly, and out of all reason and proportion. Tony must have had some good points left, or he would not have suffered the latest flame to scorch him as he had suffered it: he would not have suffered his father's knuckles between his collar and his neck. And indeed he had his good humour still. It was a blessing indeed that no amount of horsewhipping had been able to beat *that* out of him.

Yet he was sorry: the slightness of his offence galled him, as of old it must have galled those who were hanged for lambs: and the feel of those knuckles on his neck. He felt this more now than he had at the time, so much more that he could not understand how mildly he had stood it. It was his father, certainly, but —

"Constance!" muttered Tony, as he promptly blew out the candle. He had heard a stealthy foot upon the stairs; there now came a cautious tap at the door; he did not answer it.

"You're in, I know," said a voice through the door; "you're locked in."

"Oh, it's *you*!" he cried, flinging open the door; and the relighted candle revealed Winnie in her dressing-gown.

"Yes — I thought I'd come and say goodnight. Do you mind much, Tony? I mustn't stop a minute — I daren't."

"Delighted, old girl. Shut the door and take the armchair — Get out, Felix, you little skunk!"

32

"No, I mustn't stop, really."

"Frightened of being contaminated, I see!"

"Oh, Tony! You know I'm not like that!"

"*I* don't know; you girls must think pretty meanly of me: you can't help doing: suppose you'd like me the immaculate eikon style."

"*I* wouldn't, anyway, Tony."

"Well, perhaps you wouldn't, I was only joking. But it's no joke, either. I don't say I wasn't at fault; but it wasn't bad enough to deserve all that; and by Jove I think I was very good to stand it!"

"You were. I suppose Trull and Prentiss are discharged."

"Yes, worse luck; we know what it means. But look here, I'm not going on standing it. I've had enough to last me a few days. Between ourselves I mean to clear out for a bit, and I'm glad you came up, because I'll be off before breakfast."

"Where to?" returned Winnie.

"Perhaps Cambridge,"

"But surely there are no men up now?"

"There may be one or two. I shall be one if I go. I don't say I *am* going there — it might be Newmarket — but I don't say I'm not."

He was sitting on the edge of a small table, refilling his pipe. Winnie was standing near the chimney-piece, looking at him sadly.

"I wish you wouldn't be away so much!" she said.

"Well, there's not much inducement to stay here, now is there?"

"There's Camilla."

"Ah, I heard the governor brought a Portuguese cousin back here with him. How many have we, by the way?"

"Only Camilla. You ought to see her."

33

"Time enough if she's likely to stay here for a year."

"Well, she's simply lovely; I can tell you that much."

Now Tony had turned his back, and was rummaging in a drawer; and having come therein upon a photograph which had a particular attraction for him, he was regarding it, at the moment, too intently to reply.

"She is beautiful," repeated Winnie.

"Ah, so Prentise tells me," he answered indifferently; for his taste in beauty was preoccupied just then by the photograph that met his eyes.

"I'll say good night," said Winnie, rather abruptly; and as she turned round the room to him he drove home the drawer, with the photograph in it.

"Good night, then," he said, nodding.

"But you say it's to be goodbye!"

Winnie was holding up to him her pursed lips and clear pink cheek. He stooped to kiss the cheek, but drew back, and patted it instead.

"No, I'm not saying goodbye to you; I'll see you in the morning; you're always up, you know."

Winnie went away without more words. She was hurt; the tears were on her flushed cheeks when she reached the door. And Tony was left wondering why he had been such a brute as to hurt her. However, the question changed form: in a very few minutes he wanted to know why he had been such a fool. Putting it in this light, he was able to reopen the drawer he had closed in a hurry, to interest himself more freely than before in the photograph he so much admired, and entirely to forget poor Winnie, and even the Rector's knuckles against his neck.

"A jolly handsome girl," he muttered, at last, to the photograph, righteously, "and no mistake about you; now I wonder where the Cleopatra Company's performing this week?"

The photograph that fascinated him was, in fact, that of Cleopatra herself — a person who, though she had lived in ancient times, would have had considerable reason to feel indebted to Mr Pontifex's horsewhip — though of that reformer of character the chances are she had never heard.

# Chapter IV: *Untitled*

"Tea or coffee, Camilla?" enquired Constance attentively, at breakfast next morning.

"It makes no difference," answered Camilla, with a shrug hardly perceptible yet admirably expressive of indifference; "I do not care."

"But what do you generally take?" asked Constance, smiling; and the Rector, looking up from his letters, awaited the reply with visible animation.

"Oh, I take generally wine."

""Exactly!" exclaimed Mr Pontifex, fixing on his niece an eye of perhaps unconscious austerity; "you took it at the hotel yesterday morning. Your father has been so long out of England as seemingly to have forgotten English customs. It is *not* customary in England to have wine on the breakfast table. And here, Camilla, I may as well tell you that you will never see it on the table at all; I will not have it in the house!"

Camilla should have coloured; but the only person to do so was Winnie, who could not help feeling ashamed. Camilla did indeed feel troubled, but it was the matter of her uncle's premeditated speech, not its manner, that troubled her. One need not, perhaps, go to Portugal to find a really nice girl who would yet be secretly dismayed by the prospect of nothing to drink at meals but water, and water to [add to] it; still, only a foreigner would have betrayed her feelings as frankly as Camilla did now.

"That is extraordinary!" she cried, using an over-worked word of her limited vocabulary; but using it with such transparent ingenuousness that even Mr Pontifex made allowances, and observed not unkindly:

"There are many things here in England which may strike

36

you as extraordinary just at first; but I think the tables will be turned if ever you go back to Spain on a visit."

"So it is either tea or coffee," added Constance briskly. "Which will you have?"

"Then I take *caffé*; but it is all the same; it makes no matter."

Nor did the incident in itself make much matter to Camilla. Visions of wineless meals, for a whole year most likely, disturbed her more. And the only words of her uncle which stuck unpleasantly were "if you ever go back to Spain on a visit." He meant Portugal, of course. His words translated themselves into Portuguese, and Camilla wondered whether he had an idea that she might never go back. She supposed such an idea, and she tried to share it, just to see what the feeling was like. And the feeling was so miserable that she spent an hour of the forenoon in writing to her father, not miserably at all, but in Portuguese: the mere use of her own language eased her heart before it had begun to ache really badly; and proved ever after a tender cure for homesickness. She wrote in her own room, "fixed up" there by Winnie, who afterwards repaired to the school-room. The school-room, which clung to its ancient name as school-rooms will, was quite the most pleasant room in the Rectory. It was on the ground floor, at the end of the house, and as far asunder from the Rector's study as it possibly could be; and the other great merit was its own private door leading into the garden. It was prettily and simply decorated, by the hand of Constance, who was good at these things; and Constance, having performed her house-keeping duties, was sitting in the midst of her handiwork — engaged in adding to it, by colouring a tiny wicker table with a popular paint — when Winnie entered.

"Come and tell me what you think of this," she said to

Winnie, who would much rather have had the thing plain, but greatly preferred not to say so.

"I think it will be very nice."

"Nice! as if it was something to eat! I detest that word, Winnie, and you're always using it."

"Well, what do you want me to say?"

"Whether you prefer it as it was or as it's going to be — whether you don't think it'll look much more artistic presently than it ever looked before."

"Candidly, I liked it better as it was; but I'm not artistic, you know."

"You are not, certainly," said Constance drily, "and I might have known quite well what you would say. If it wasn't for me this room would be a pig-sty! I only hope Camilla has some sense of what's artistic. What have you done with her, by the way?"

"She is writing a letter."

"Writing already! Her impressions, I suppose; or perhaps to ask her father to write and order her wine! I must say I think the Rector was very good-natured over that business at breakfast; don't you?"

"Well, to tell you the truth," said Winnie, with some reluctance, "I thought he said far more than there was any necessity to say!"

Constance was seated near the window. The sun touched her light pretty hair almost to golden, and displayed her uncommonly good profile to even uncommon advantage, as she glanced sharply across the room, her lips pursed and the paint-brush poised over her work. Her glance rested on Winnie, under whose solid weight the rocking-chair was groaning, while her strong hands lay idle in her lap, and her whole attitude — and appearance, at the moment — lacked distinction.  Constance, on the other hand, though always busy with something, would contrive always to look pretty as well, and brisk, and neat.  Nor could anyone be nicer than she could who objected to that epithet.  The pity was that she was not always nice, and that when nasty she was nastiest to Winnie — whose words and looks now alike excited her scorn.

"I do think, Winnie," said she at length, "that your way of criticising what Father says,  even between ourselves, is in the very worst taste!"

Taste was a very strong point with Constance.  Also, she was just as much in the habit — the perfectly respectful habit — of speaking of their father as "the Rector", as Tony and Winnie were; so that the more strictly filial expression was in itself a reproof and a snub.

"I don't see any harm in it," said Winnie, calmly.  "I think too much was said, and surely there's no harm in saying what one thinks?  Camilla has evidently been used to wine, and she should have it here."

"For breakfast?" inquired Constance blandly.

"For dinner, at all events.  This is the only house I ever knew where wine wasn't on the table for those who took it."

"You have known so many!"

"It makes me ashamed," said Winnie, apparently without noticing the sneer, "to set people down to cold water as we do; and it made me ashamed to hear the Rector speak like that about wine, on Camilla's first morning too!"

"If I were you," retorted Constance, "I should be ashamed to say so, that's all!  I don't know how you can, when you see with your own eyes, every day too, the consequences of drink: when you see families ruined by it, even in our little village: when you couldn't look at a paper — supposing you ever *did* look at one — without being appalled by the crimes and misery it causes: and when — and when you have poor Tony continually before you!"

"Now don't be ridiculous about Tony," exclaimed Winnie, moved at last; "he is not so 'poor' as that!"

"So I *know*!"

"Then perhaps you know where he has gone to now?  He must have left the house before we were up."

"I don't wonder — after last night!"

"But where has he gone?"

"Perhaps — perhaps to Cambridge."

"So likely! When every soul has gone down.  No; I should be glad to be sure it wasn't Newmarket; I should be thankful indeed if I were quite sure about that."

Winnie had already flushed hotly, but at the name of Newmarket her flush deepened, for an obvious reason.  She jumped up clumsily, her soft eyes flashing, and sought to hide her confusion in an outburst of generous indignation very unusual in the mild, easy-going girl.

"It is hateful of you, Constance, to speak of Tony as you do continually!  You would not do it to his face, then how dare you behind his back?  He has his faults, and no one knows them better than he does.  Whatever they are, he has never been anything but kind and generous to us both, and he speaks very kindly of *you* behind your back — I can tell you that — little as you deserve it!  And oh! Constance, you put me in a passion when you speak of him so; yet there are things about him that trouble me too; and they trouble me all the more because he is so good to me.  He *is* good, say what you like; you don't know the best of him as I do!"

"My impression is," said Constance, who had borne her rebuke with ostentatious patience, "that we none of us know the worst of him!  If he is betting and gambling he is pretty

40

certain to be in debt. You haven't noticed, I suppose, that he never wears his watch now? Well, we may be prepared for anything, and when everything has come out you may be sorry you lost your temper with me for doing what you yourself say there is no harm in — saying what one thinks."

"I am sorry for that already," said humble Winnie. "But you know as well as I do that poor Tony has never had a fair chance at home. And now the Rector has flown from one extreme to the other — doesn't mind what he does, as long as he doesn't do it here — and makes neither complaint nor inquiry about his goings away or his comings home. Yet last night, for a mere trifle, he creates such a scene as would make *me* ten times worse, if *I* were Tony!"

"*I* shouldn't call it a trifle," said Constance decidedly; "I should call it anything *but* a trifle, to sit gambling and drinking with the men."

But Winnie let her have the last word, which, indeed, was the only thing to do with Constance; and for some time there was silence in the school-room, save for the crackle of the wicker table, under the infliction of a tasteful tint. Winnie was in the rocking-chair again, idle as before, but not rocking it now; nor was her expression so contented. However, she had occasion to colour with pleasure before long, nor could she avoid doing so, when a step was heard on the gravel outside and a young fellow in flannels appeared at the window. It was not the truant Tony, but a smaller, darker, better-looking young man — in fact, a vexatiously handsome boy — who leant in through the windows and greeted the girls with a gentlemanly restraint which was his inoffensive mannerism.

"Good morning, ladies."

"Well, Erskine! good morning," said the girls together.

The young man, beaming through the window as far as he

could, was peering by turns into every corner of the room. "Where is she?" he asked *sotto voce*.

"Who?" said Constance, looking up swiftly from her task.

"The new arrival."

"How do you know there is a new arrival?"

"I told him," Winnie confessed.

"Really!" Constance laughed. "And when was your last clandestine meeting — you two — eh?"

"In what you will consider a shocking vulgar place, Constance," answered the young fellow, with great gravity: "over the hen-yard wall, at feeding-time yesterday afternoon, as I rode by."

"You never told me you had seen Erskine, Winnie!"

"My dear," replied Winnie, with a sprightliness she had not exhibited while they were alone, "I never tell you when I have seen the sun. He favours us with the light of his countenance most days during the summer; and so does Erskine. Yesterday I never saw you go out — you were so long, you know — therefore it's no wonder you saw neither the sun nor Erskine — for once!"

"We're getting clever," said Constance; but Erskine murmured a gentlemanly "Good old Winnie!" (strictly a 'Varsity phrase at this time), and asked if he was not to hear what the new arrival was like, since apparently they couldn't or wouldn't produce her.

"Like?" said Constance. "She's uncommon, certainly. And she just misses being very pretty."

"Misses!" cried Winnie. "She *is* pretty, and more than pretty; she's simply lovely, Erskine!"

The young man in the window glanced from one sister to the other as if to remind them that he knew them both well enough to draw a line of pretty accurate deduction between their respective opinions on any given point or person. But his glance was full of interest, and of intelligence too; which, however, was not to be mistaken for downright intellect, to which the handsome young gentleman would have been the last person in the world to lay a claim.

"I'm immensely interested, I must own," he answered them. "And is she tremendously Spanish, and all that? and does she talk broken English?"

"No," declared Winnie.

"Well, — fractured," amended Constance. "There are some bad cracks in the English as yet, and the words that come easiest to her she seems inclined to work to death. But there *is* something rather delightful about her, and really, Erskine, I'm quite curious to know what you will think of her."

"Well, I'm curious too."

"Then why don't you come in and sit down? The door's within six feet of you. Come in and be patient."

Erskine looked at his watch. "No, I can only stay five minutes longer; I've got to meet Dr Underwood at twelve, at the dispensary, about a match he wants me to play in. By the way, I'm playing cricket all tomorrow, so the chances are I shan't behold this interesting cousin of yours before Sunday. Well, I'll be in church without fail."

Constance shook her head and looked grave. "I'm afraid it doesn't follow that you'll see her *there*."

"Why? Isn't she Church?"

Constance explained what she was; but the young gentleman received the information without visible revulsion. On the other hand, he expressed indifference, and incurred one of those neat little reproofs which Constance was in the habit of administering to her old friends. He might not profess to be religious; he might even manage to lead a good life (in other respects) without going regularly to church; but not to be alive to the great gulf fixed between religion and idolatry was to stand himself on the wrong side of the gulf, and as bad, if not worse than the idolatries. This Constance pointed out at some length, and no doubt conclusively, though Erskine was smoothing the smiles from his delicate moustache when the door opened and the idolater herself appeared upon the scene. For a moment she stood still in the doorway, evidently taken aback; but the next, she advanced boldly upon the young man in the window, with a frank smile and her hand outstretched.

Constance, for one, was scandalised, but did what she could for the situation by ejaculating a hasty introduction. Whereupon Camilla turned to her very nervously, and stammered out:

"I — I thought it was Antonio!"

For a moment they all considered. Then Winnie said, "Oh! Tony! I have been telling her about Tony!" And then they all laughed, Camilla innocently endeavouring to hide her confusion in merriment; and the ice was broken.

The girls explained that Erskine, though not own brother to them, was "almost as bad as one." As for him, he could not take his eyes off her, and it was the easier not to do so as his back was to the strong light. Winnie was right: for once her generous enthusiasm had not got the better of her judgement: and what had been lovely in her simple eyes was lovely to him in his more sophisticated ones. Certainly Camilla's confusion did not distract from her good looks; it gave her colour, in which she was naturally deficient; it added lustre to her southern eyes; it animated her as she had not been animated since her arrival at the Rectory. The laughter was good. It left smiles behind it, as a splash leaves ripples.

The young man who was not Antonio inquired about the voyage and the Bay of Biscay, recounted his own experience of those nutritious waters, and was particularly polite and pleasant and conversational in the too few minutes left him. But at twelve he went. He was obliged to go, or the cricketing doctor would do so, who was to be seen at the dispensary in the matter of tomorrow's match. And Winnie got up and unblushingly granted his request to her to escort him off the premises; for was he not as bad as their brother? So Camilla was left alone with Constance, and no sooner were the other two out of earshot than she exclaimed eagerly:

"Who is he? I do not understand."

"Erskine Hope — at least that's his name, but it won't convey anything, as Winnie has hardly had time to sing his praises to you, yet. She will before long. Well then, he's the young Squire here: owns all the property — all but *our* little bits — and came into it when he came of age, last year. He's at Oxford now, is as amiable as he looks, and thinks more about a game called cricket than anything else. When he isn't at Oxford he's with his mother — Lady Harriett Hope — either here or in London; he's all she has, or has ever had since her husband died when the boy was a baby; and I must say he's a model son. There! Now what do you think of him?"

"I think," said Camilla, "he is a very pretty man."

"A *what* man?"

Instead of repeating the epithet, Camilla exclaimed with good-humoured conviction: "I have said a nonsense!""

"Well, very nearly one," said Constance, smiling presently; "very nearly *two* nonsenses"

And she explained them both, quite kindly, and Camilla took the explanations most gratefully to heart. She was intensely anxious to learn to speak English properly; and

45

Constance, who was the very person to coach her effectively, if she liked, and she evinced a pleasing disposition to take trouble to do so. The two got on excellently during the hour that was left to them before luncheon; but Constance was ever at her best when you had her to yourself — unless you happened to be Winnie. Her temper had improved: she was the victim of her peculiar temper, and had the extenuating misfortune of being perfectly well aware of its peculiarity. Good-nature came naturally to Winnie, but not to Constance; and to a galling consciousness of the contrast between them — to the unfair but comprehensible feeling, that Winnie was more lovable than she by reason of qualities that were minute, and therefore no credit to her — may be ascribed much of the elder sister's habitual treatment of the younger. Yet it is difficult to make out a brief for the defence of natures — in themselves so essentially difficult. Their angles bruise not only the innocent offender, but the innocent who does not offend at all. Thus, even this morning, Camilla was hurt as no ordinary person could have hurt one in her special circumstance. The table was finished; Camilla, asked for her opinion, had approved of it (no doubt sincerely, as she had an inherent love of colour); but, in bending to inspect, some amber beads, part of a necklet, rolled over her collar and sparkled in the sun, catching Constance's attention.

"Why, what on earth do you wear a necklace for during the day?" cried she, at once.

"I wear it always," answered Camilla, raising her head in haste, so that the beads were out of sight again in a moment.

"But *why*, child?"

"I do not know. It is in our country a custom. We in Lisbon do not think it extraordinary. We consider it lucky for the girls to wear them always."

"Lucky!" said Camilla scornfully. "Who gave you the thing, pray?"

"My mother fastened it round my neck before I can remember. I would not take it off for the world, because if I did I would have no more peace."

Constance would have said no more, but for the last sentence. This made such a course impossible — to Constance.

"Camilla, Camilla, this is dreadful!" she exclaimed, sincerely enough, but with as little tact as taste. It is ignorance and superstition, and nothing less! As for the religion which teaches you that peace and happiness are dependent upon charms and amulets, it is no religion at all, and the sooner you can see that, the better it will be for you and the more thankful we shall feel!"

Some sufferers would have made a touching scene of it. But Camilla, though sensitive, was not sentimental. She simply answered:

"I cannot help it. In my country it is the custom; but it has nothing to do with our religion. You see you do not understand, and I cannot make you, so what can we do?"

She bent her head to one side and shrugged her shoulders in her own peculiar and delicate foreign fashion; but to Constance there was a suggestion of indifference in any shrug, and she was on the point of an exhaustive rejoinder when the gong rang and mercifully put an end to the discussion.

# Chapter V: *Untitled*

Camilla had hit off Erskine Hope with unconscious precision and felicity in her comic phrase, "a pretty man". He was one. Much as he would have hated to hear it, the ignoble epithet defined him, at least in outline. He had been a pretty boy, with dark-blue eyes lintelled by the blackest eye-brows at Eton; and he could not be acquitted of prettiness merely because a third eye-brow flourished on his upper lip. He could not help it; it was his misfortune, not his own doing; and to suppose him effeminate just because he was better-looking than you or I — better-looking than we would care to be, if you wish it that way — would be to suppose what was emphatically not the case. He had gone through Eton, certainly, with a feminist nickname, which stuck to him like a burr both then and at Oxford (and there is occasionally insight the most profound in these same boyish nicknames, some of which might well serve as life-long labels); but "Mary" Hope had twice played against Harrow at Lord's, notwithstanding, and had been within a place of playing against Cambridge for the last two seasons. He was a cricketer. His manhood is established in that word. Yet it is a fact that he neither despised nor affected to despise the society of girls. Indeed, he liked them; and admitted it, which is surely another mark of the man.

The taste was inherited. Lady Harriett was never so happy, in Erskine's absences, as when surrounded by a bevy of silly young girls; nor did her exemplary son make it impossible for her to indulge this whim in his vacations. He shared it, within bounds — the bounds of a most precious discretion and exceptionally good sense. He was a brother to the girls; a splendid brother, infinitely more obliging and delightful than the enthusiastic thing was ever known to be. So the house in town shimmered and rustled every year with the perpetual flutter of very young women; and the young women as a rule availed themselves of certain advantages which Lady Harriett put within their reach; so that very seldom could the same young women be brought together two years in succession. In fact, Lady Harriett had extravagantly married every girl who had the smallest claim on her of kinship or connection; had run through her nieces, of every consanguineous hue, before Erskine came of age; and had this year accompanied him into the country otherwise unattended, quite bankrupt at last in the companionship wherein her cheerful old heart delighted. However, there were the Pontifex girls in the country. They had never visited Lady Harriett in town, because Mr Pontifex would not let them; nor was Lady Harriett sure that she should enjoy having Constance; but it was pleasant to have them at hand in the country — they were young girls. And Erskine was on his soft fraternal terms with them. Winnie was merely his favourite sister of the whole tribe; had always been so; yet never a sign of nonsense between them; and if nonsense should ultimately intrude, what then? The Pontifexes were an even older County family than the Hopes; the present head of the family, with all his peculiarities had not only good blood in his veins but good money well invested; and as for Winnie, everybody liked her, and Lady Harriett — who dealt in love, not in liking — loved her dearly. It was not, perhaps, a feeling of deep root, for which the old lady had not indeed the spiritual soil; but it was sincere, as far as it went; otherwise it must have perished at the first breath of a suspicion which Lady Harriett had quite lately inhaled: a suspicion that there was *not* such safety as she had hitherto fancied — on Winnie's side.

Certainly when he asked her to see him off the premises, after his first mere glimpse of Camilla, the girl had complied with an alacrity which enriched her complexion. This was already richly tinted by sunshine and fresh air; and a glare suited it as it suited her hair; in short, Winnie looked not only radiant, but positively pretty, as she sauntered down the drive at Erskine's side. So the pretty man did not happen to give her a glance. His mortal eyes were on the gravel in front of him: the eternal pair wrestled with the fresh face, which was slipping from before them, feature by feature. And when he spoke it was to inform Winnie that of course *she* was right — he didn't mention in what.

"You mean about Camilla?"

"Of course!"

"There!" cried Winnie, in triumph. "I *knew* you'd be on my side about Camilla! Now give me your honest opinion: isn't she lovely? don't you think she's the loveliest girl you ever saw in your life?"

Erskine did think so; but he would not have owned up to that thought for anything. It was his gentlemanly habit to keep the expression of his opinion well within restraint, and this came the more easily to him, if anything, when the expressed opinion was a good one. Nor is this merely a polite way of mentioning that he was ashamed to betray enthusiasm; the truth is that that sort of thing did not come easily to him; and the so-called "good form" for which he had a reputation up at Oxford was, in his case at least, instinctive and not acquired. It is the more necessary to insist on this because fine manners are made as well as born, but are much more excusable when born, as in the case of this young gentleman; who, instead of praising hastily where he hastily admired, picked an allowable hole or two, incurring Miss

Winnie's frank displeasure.

"You are hard to please, Erskine: you always were...."

Erskine smiled, and didn't know that he was. The vision was fading. He had lost the expression, the smile, already. He did not mean to lose the dark southern eyes; and indeed, they had lodged securely in his brain.

"I suppose it's because she's a Catholic," said Winnie irately

"Pity you can't get Constance to suppose that too," he answered quietly.

"Ah, Constance! I thought you were on my side, but really you seem to have gone over to hers. Do you know, I thought she was going to let out something."

"What was that?"

"I'm afraid you'd make fun or tell some one; and it wouldn't be kind to do either."

"Then don't tell *me*."

So she told him on the spot — about finding Camilla fast asleep on her knees, with a coloured print of "Nossa Senhora" (as she had this morning confessed to Winnie) half hidden by her clasped hands, and half by her hair. They were such very old cronies, these two: she could not help telling him what touched her so genuinely. If it touched him too he certainly did not show it. He appeared more moved on discovering, by a question, how it was that Constance had not seen the picture too.

"You're a good sort, Winnie!" he exclaimed, almost impulsively, as his hand slid into one of its own size, very nearly. This was at the gate, where they said good morning, having for once met and parted without talking cricket — his strong point, and hers too, but in another sense. She had a very happy, flushed, delighted face when she got back to the house; indeed it was her unreasonable happiness that restrained her from returning just then to the school-room and Constance.

Meanwhile Erskine Hope had turned to the right and was proceeding on his way down the village, hardly recognising the familiar figures that saluted him with forefinger or knee, according to sex, as he passed; though he mechanically acknowledged their somewhat servile civilities. He was plainly preoccupied; but not with the thought of her who was just then thinking of him. The fresh face was before him still, but in a new setting — one of dark hair in an impossible tangle — and with closed eyelids and white fingers locked beneath the cheek. The little coloured print burnt like fire within the bedevilled hair; and altogether the imagined picture was much more easily caught hold of with the mind's eye, than the remembered one. Where the other eye beheld the adipose figure of Dr Underwood, in the shadow of his dog-cart outside the Dispensary door, the bathos within the young man's skull was grotesque, and he laughed. The necessary final arrangings with that keen though corpulent cricketer apparently dissipated the vision that ought not to be named in the same breath; in fact, it did; for Erskine was no more addicted to visions, in the ordinary way, than he was to enthusiasms, and he had plenty to say to the only other inhabitant (a dirty old gentleman in a smock-frock and one of Erskine's own silk hats) whom he encountered in the few yards between the Dispensary and the Hall.

For the Hall was peculiarly situated, as Halls go, in the country. It was built in the village street as the average London mansion is to the pavement; and of such, indeed, was its general style. Spiked iron palings guarded the lower windows, and the space between was severely flagged. In a village so faultlessly idyllic, in other respects, it was out of place, to say the least of it, and raised the speculation suggested by the fly in the amber — to no better purpose. However, it had two sides, and this was the bad one. The other side was very good indeed. You turned your back upon the rustic street and knocked — with a town-bred knocker — at a front-door whose existence outside the four-mile radius was a cockney impertinence. But depression ended, and delight began, with that repulsive portal once closed behind you; for over against it, across the hall, was another door — a garden-door, in perfect keeping with the miniature paradise on which it opened. And compared with the house, the garden it concealed so cleverly was a little paradise indeed. The close-cropped lawn was shadowed by noble elms; the yew hedges beyond seemed all from one mould; the flower-beds in the hedged square were individually like fancy cakes in a master confectioner's; and their collective arrangement was one of the kaleidoscope; and the thatched summer-house at the end of the long walk was a summer-house to dream of — and to ache from if you sat too long on the quaint, tortuous seats. Thus, though the Hall itself was not of much account, the Hall garden was quite perfect in its way. If it was a theatrical way, rather, as if the garden smacked slightly of the set scene, neither Erskine nor his mother discerned the taint; and as for Lady Harriett, a greedy theatre-goer, this would have been no taint at all, but a positive recommendation. As it was she cherished a very pretty affection for her old garden. Its rather obvious beauties charmed her soul and quite satisfied her sense of the beautiful. And the sun seldom shone for any length of time without casting her substantial shadow on the well-kept paths; save when she spent an afternoon under the thatched roof of the summer-house, in a comfortable chair carried there expressly for the reception of her person, which indeed demanded special arrangements.

She was in the garden when Erskine returned from the Rectory, but not in the summer-house. She was promenading by herself among the fancy flower-beds in the square whose sides were yew hedges. From the garden door he saw through the trees, and just over the clean-cut hedge beyond, her white hair gleaming in the sun; and ten seconds later he had planted a kiss beneath it on the good-natured face. For the young fellow's natural undemonstrativeness was charmingly heightened by the perpetual contrast — that of an unrestrained and unashamed affection for the jolly old woman his mother.

"Well?" said Lady Harriett, with amused subtlety in her good natured tone.

"Well, I've just to say [I've] seen her."

"Tell me what you think of her."

Erskine drew his mother's plump hand within his arm and sauntered at her side. Some steps were taken in silence. And as for his answer when it came, do we not already know his first impression of Camilla Pontifex? Enough to add that he was in the habit of giving his impressions more frankly to Lady Harriett than to any other souls; but that in this case he was a shade less frank with her than was his wont. However, he said enough for his mother presently to rejoin:

"I say, I hope you don't mean to fall in love with her!"

"I!"

"Yes, you."

"My dear old lady," laughed Erskine, recovering himself, "you might remember a fellow's age!"

"I do. You're not quite twenty-three. So that's too old to make a fool of oneself, is it?"

"Too young, dear mother, to marry."

"Nonsense! You look older than you are, and looks are everything. You have a moustache, and though I am thankful to say that you shave every morning, your chin turns blue before night. No, you're neither too old nor too young — nor too young-looking — to make a fool of yourself. What's more you're blushing!"

"You're enough to make a saint blush, you wicked old woman," said Erskine, laughing again. "To think you can't trust a fellow after all these years: and all those cousins: to say nothing of Pontifex girls!"

"Ah, poor Winnie!"

"Now what on earth are you pitying her for?"

"I see a little disappointment in the distance!"

Erskine became actually excited. He waved his disengaged hand, in a way that would have astonished his friends, while he affirmed, in clipped but potent phrases, that there had never been anything of *that* sort between him and Winnie. It was a shame to hint at it, even in fun. They were the oldest chums. They understood one another perfectly. And hang it, you didn't fall in love with a girl you had been a brother to all your life!

"Perhaps not," thought Lady Harriett, "but she may fall in love with you. He doesn't see this. He *is* very young, after all!"

Aloud, however, she merely laughed at him; which rather irritated the model son; so that he essayed to veer the subject.

"Talking of Winnie, she has a pretty story about the Portuguese girl," he remarked, referring with a fine indifference (not lost upon his mother) to both girls in one breath. "She's a Catholic, you must know."

"That's interesting!" exclaimed the ungodly Lady Harriett, "I

55

wonder they have her at the Rectory. What's the story?"

"Well, now think of it, I haven't to tell any one."

"So your mother's any one, is she?"

He told her promptly, and the tears were in her eyes a moment. She was one of those good-natured, emotional women who are as easily touched as amused, and she enjoyed a tear or two quite as much as a good laugh. The pathos required was not of a very subtle order; nor the humour either, though she herself was humorous,

"I will call there tomorrow while you are playing cricket," she said, as they went in to luncheon, trailing across the lawn arm-in-arm, "and I'll ask the whole tribe of them to dinner. Of course Mr Pontifex will refuse; but as usual he will mumble something about our going there instead; and for once I shall take him at his word. There shall be a dinner-party either there or here; and I think it will be better there."

"Teetotal drinks!" said Erskine warningly.

"We must survive them. I want to see something of the girl, and I think she may like to see something of me, for how they may treat a Catholic at the Rectory I simply shudder to imagine!"

The shudder, however, was not visible, and a smile was. For her continuing and prospective state of bereavement, as regarded young girls, was a real trial to the good gregarious lady. And here was a young girl! From Erskine's account, which was amplified at luncheon, she was the very girl for whom Lady Harriett's soul was pining, and with regard to that young man, after all he would only admire as he had admired before. He admired often; but he had given comfortable proof that he was not susceptible; and it was a queer thing, said his mother (as she settled herself for her afternoon nap), if he could not take care of himself once more as successfully as he had taken care of himself on fifty former occasions.

So the call duly came off; and so did the invitation to dine at the Rectory, which was accepted with an alacrity little short of indecent. The Rector looked more than usually grim over it, for of course he had not dreamt of an acceptance at all, as Lady Harriett very well knew. She did not stay long after achieving her object; for the Rector would monopolise her when she called, and they disliked one another. That was why he did it, to save the girls from pollution by the private conversation of a woman whom he had once called "worldly" to her face. He let them go to see her sometimes; for it was necessary not to quarrel; but he also let Lady Harriett understand that they should never wear the shoes of the empty little flirts her nieces. The presence of Camilla, and probably the outrageous acceptance of his foolish invitation, made him doubly forbidding; and when tea had been taken, and the little dinner-party arranged for an evening of the following week, the caller was glad enough to go.

Then the Rector also vanished; and it was discovered that the visitor had made an immense impression upon Camilla; who had not exchanged a dozen words with her, though she had met the old lady's interested eyes more than once, and felt them all the time. What she had been most struck with was the old lady's charming white hair; and on her saying so Constance betrayed signs of titillation.

"What do you laugh at?" asked Camilla, prepared to hear that she had uttered "another nonsense".

"At you admiring her hair so."

"Why, is it not pretty?"

"Oh yes, it's pretty; and it's her own, too; only it was as dark as yours a year ago — that's all!"

"Do you mean to say it is possible that she — that she

57

*paints* it?"

Constance laughed. "Dyes it, my dear! No, she doesn't dye it now; that's just it; she *used* to dye it when it was dark. And only fancy, it was quite a young man, living near here, who persuaded her to give up dyeing her hair — and she's old enough to be his mother! Now I think of it, we'll have him to dinner the same evening. You ought to know him. He has a great influence over some people — Lady Harriett for one, and the Rector rather likes him, in spite of his being High Church; but *I* think he is just the queerest creature in the world!"

Is it necessary to say that Constance was referring, satirically as usual, to a young ritualistic rector who had called on the afternoon preceding Camilla's arrival?

# Chapter VI: Essingham All Souls

James Pontifex made haste to exchange letters with his brother. He wanted to hear of Camilla, even more than from her, and he mentioned business delays which would defer alike his visit to Essingham and his departure from England. The Rector replied, ignoring business matters, but reporting favourably, if somewhat coldly, upon Camilla; he did add, however, that he hoped James had made up his mind to leave her where she was. James, as we know, had that desire, and the remark did much in moulding it to intention — more even than Camilla's own perfectly satisfactory letters. She was always writing, and had hurried but affectionate answers from Glasgow, Manchester and Birmingham, all in the first week; the energetic gentleman rushing from centre to centre over his purchases of "plant". In each she was instructed to say candidly if she was unhappy; but she read another entreaty between the lines; nor was she, for one moment, unhappy enough to sit down and say so in cold ink. She might have been happier in Lisbon, it was true; but that was another matter, one for a private shrug, not for the unnecessary botheration of one already over-bothered business man. Besides, he knew it, and it was for her good that he wished her to spend in England the term of his own transportation. The one thing they had agreed to recognise as a barrier, was the semblance of an aversion, on Camilla's part, from the Rectory or its inmates. But she wrote with enthusiasm of the place, and very kindly of the people. She stood in awe of the Rector, as yet; but meant to grow out of that. Constance was kind. Winnie she liked better. As for the man cousin, she had not so much as seen him, but it would matter very little what *he* was like, as it appeared he was very seldom at home.

This was perfectly sincere, if unconsciously coloured by a good girl's knowledge of her father's wishes. Still, Camilla was not one to be made miserable with a word or a look. Amiable in herself, she was slow to take offence from another — slower than the English girl of equal amiability. If as sensitive, she was less touchy; but perhaps she was not *quite* so sensitive. For the Portuguese are a philosophic people, who take their troubles for the most part with a shrug and a cigarette: and open reference to her "nonsenses", to the wickedness of wine, and to her religion itself, were burdens which Camilla easily dislodged with the national shrug. Their momentary weight was forgotten, nor would its recollection have made her ache. Constance's remarks *á propos* of her necklace were the heaviest yet, but soon they were a trifle not worth thinking about — at any rate not worth writing about, when there were so many things which it was a daily delight merely to chronicle.

At seventeen one is readily delighted, and the more readily in strange surroundings. Camilla's delights began each morning when the maid drew up her blind, and she woke to behold from her pillow the dark-green elm-tops rocking and trembling against the blue sky. The five slothful moments she found it safe to indulge in here were as good, in their way, as any five of the day. Luckily that was a fine August; there were moments when the sky looked actually as blue as the one she had left; and every day there was intense heat, in which Camilla revelled, and not the less heartily because others complained. It was the first point on which she felt herself enviable in English eyes, but the sensation itself was enviable. The shining sun, of course, gilded most things, but some few would have seemed golden under the most sombre conditions — in the eyes of foreign seventeen [year-olds]. Among these were the long walks with Winnie and the dogs on the warren, and the pine plantations, and far from fence or hedge: the visiting of villagers with Constance, who scolded them if they wanted it, and left tracts whether they wanted them or not: rudimentary lessons in lawn-tennis (an "extraordinary" game, she said) under Winnie for choice: and *not* a like initiation into the craft of bagatelle, under the Rector, with Constance looking. Yet this last went into a letter, and delighted James Pontifex as much as it had frightened Camilla. Erskine Hope, too, who frequently adorned the stage, and proved as pleasant as he was "pretty", was no product of the weather; but many words were not wasted on *him*, though he received due mention.

Constance was voted a trump (in effect — for of course this correspondence was conducted in Portuguese) for the pains she took to improve one's English — never failing to point out a nonsense — and also for showing one the things of local interest. These were various. There were Roman remains — coins and camps (about which, certainly, Camilla did not rave) and a brace of sarcophagi in the very garden. A flint-knapper followed his quaint, antique calling hard by, and she had nearly chopped off her finger-ends in trying her hand at it. She had seen the ditch in which a village father had lately cut his throat — through drink; Constance, indeed, had shown her the place and told her the story more than once. And lastly there were the two churches, All Souls' and St John's — two churches between four hundred souls! They stood at each end of the village, which had formerly comprised two parishes; but All Souls' — whose graveyard adjoined the Rectory garden — had long ago fallen into disuse and decay. Camilla explored both within the week; there was no occasion to describe them to her father, who, of course, had been born

61

and bred in the village; but she did tell him that she considered All Souls' "extraordinary", and her favourite adjective was emphasised by being written in English. Moreover inadequacy was its only fault in this connection. Essingham All Souls' would employ an idle antiquary for a matter of weeks; from the thatched roof to the red Roman tiles in the chancel, all is wonder and interest, even to the ignoramus; and Camilla duly wondered and was interested — to some purpose. She took an opportunity of going back to poke about there by herself, Constance, whose kindness was occasionally cursory and perfunctory, having told her to do so (being herself, at the time, more anxious for tea); and it chanced that her going back resulted in two or three things which never found their way into any letter.

The afternoon of her choice was the one preceding the little dinner-party at the Rectory, when Constance was in a rare pother behind the domestic scenes, with Winnie for her well-snubbed but possibly rather incompetent lieutenant. It was by the latter's advice that Camilla had taken herself off: but her own unaided inclination had transferred the key of the old church from its nail in the hall to her pocket. However, her inclination was so far justified that for fully half an hour the crannies and curiosities of the queer old place engaged her wondering attention. The most interesting features naturally escaped her unskilled vision; but she had no mind to notice just because she had overhauled the objects of obvious interest. The spot had other attractions. The afternoon was excessively hot, and this ancient interior wore a bleached, scraped, white-washed appearance — directly due to the puritans — which was eminently cool. So instead of going, Camilla fastened herself into one of the square pews, and glued her eyes to a patch of sunlight in the chancel, and her thoughts to Portugal; with the result that the eyes were under tears in two minutes, and soft, luminous and lovely beyond the conception of her cousins — before whom she would have shed blood [rather] than a tear. This special reserve was on the whole a pity; partly because it is only womanly in a woman to weep among women, on occasion (and later, when occasions came but not a tear, Camilla was set down as somewhat indifferent, with all her sweetness; and partly because Camilla had the rare and unconscious accomplishment of crying prettily, which it was a shame for no one ever to see. Yet her philosophic instincts had something to do with this too: her tears were tranquil, because she would remember, with a shrug, that they could do no good. The story somehow affected the lachrymose duet. And she would promptly dry them. She had done so now, and dropped her handkerchief; and in stooping to pick it up she uttered an exclamation which would be considered profane if translated into English; for the amber beads of which we wot passed without warning from her neck on [to] the floor of the pew, in a ringing rattling shower.

Camilla leant forward without moving until the last bead had done spinning, and the disintegrated necklace studded the dust of years like stars reflected. She could imagine how it had happened. To prevent further remarks on the one point on which she was very sensitive, she had taken to collars, which she wore with the lower edge jammed here and there between the beads, to keep the latter out of sight. But the threading cord was very old; and in bending forward the collar had cut through it in a frayed place — as indeed was proved by examination of the cord. The precious beads lay all over the floor of the pew, that was what mattered; and Camilla was on her knees, picking them up, when a man's step rang over the flags through the stillness of the old church.

Camilla knelt upright, in a mild agony. If it was her uncle, he was the last person she would wish to know about her beads. He would be worse than Constance on the sore subject; he might take them from her. She thought, for a moment, of remaining in hiding, where she was; but happily for a moment only. Consideration decided her on the only wise course: she rose, quitted the pew, closed the door behind her, and did all so softly that she was half-way down the aisle before she was seen.

And then it was not, however, the Rector who saw her and whom she confronted as boldly as she could. It was a young man in a rather shabby suit, who greeted her with a grin and his outstretched hand, which she could not refuse.

"I might have known it was you, for the girls never come here." he said; "but I saw the door open as I passed, and I never thought of you. Jolly old church, isn't it? It's one of the oldest in England. I say, you *are* Camilla, aren't you?"

The abrupt question was prompted by the young girl's obvious confusion, which, however, she made a plucky effort to shake off. "Yes; and — you are — Tony?"

He bowed grotesquely.

"Now we know each other — better late than never. And excuse me, but it's jolly meeting you here, of all places. We don't think half enough of this rummy old ruin — for it is one — and that's *why* it's one. Has anyone shown you over it, I wonder?"

Camilla replied that Constance had; and felt, as she spoke, considerable gratitude to the young man who had put her at ease so speedily.

"Ah, Constance! She has the best head in the family, I dare say, but the antique's hardly her thing; nor mine either; but I could tell you two or three things she couldn't — if you care to know."

"I thank you," returned Camilla; "but I cannot trouble you like that. I have been here the whole afternoon. I see everything. Now I go."

"Why hurry? The girls are busy — I've been in and seen 'em. You are not required in the house."

"It is true."

"Then let me improve your mind — only don't tell them. I put it that way, or they may explain the humour of it. We'll begin with that heap of hassocks under the gallery; will you come and look at them?" Camilla assented with her expressive shoulders, and a smile, and then she followed him. "They're awfully new, these hassocks: lumps of peat cut clean out of the ground and not a thing done to them afterwards: corrects name *dosses*. Now look at the alms-box; I'll lay ten to one Constance didn't point it out to you, did she?" Camilla shook her head. "No, it's not the sort of thing to strike her; but it's Elizabethan, and three hundred years old, for all that."

"Three hundred!"

"Bless you, that's nothing! See this font? It's fourteenth-century — a hale old font of five hundred years or age!"

"It is extraordinary."

"You're right, it is *so*; but look at that window — no, not the one with the pictures — the low one on the other side. That's the oldest part of the whole show, that is. It's suspected of being Saxon, and if so, it's just about twice as old as the font."

"A thousand years! It is impossible."

"Well, if it *is* Saxon. The one with the pictures, that you were just looking at, is Norman. The old couple in the gay clothes probably built half the church with their money; and we don't even know their names!"

Camilla was now following her guide as closely with her feet as with her attention. She was pleased and interested — more pleased, on the whole. He opened a door, and she peeped in at his side. Her eyes ran up the solitary rope, but lost it halfway in the twilight, and leapt to the bells. On the left a massive ladder lacked many rungs; the beat of wings was heard high overhead as they opened the door.

"And this is the belfry tower, wherein the birds make their nests — which I've robbed before today. It makes me shudder to think of it now! I used to go up the ladder, and it's rotten as touchwood, and most likely as old as the tower itself!"

"How dreadful! I wonder ..." Camilla mused.

"Yes?"

"I wonder whether my father did such things when he was a very young man here!"

"They say he did worse: I've heard the lightning conductor outside was *his* way of getting up: he was a fine fellow, from all accounts, your father."

Camilla was pleased. To please in return, she endeavoured to express a livelier appreciation of all shewn being shown as told; though what she privately appreciated much more was his genial way of telling her. Not that he bored her in the least. His touch as showman was as light as it was rapid. Five minutes from the start saw him in the mouldy pulpit, pointing out traces of the rood-screen; and in the vault underneath were time-beaten volumes, smelling of another century, which called forth an unofficial truth from Tony. "Think of these books left here since this church was last used — years and years ago! But my father doesn't take the slightest interest in this one, as you may imagine. He doesn't put his money in it from year's end to year's end. He isn't half keen enough about this world's treasures, in my humble opinion.

66

You've seen the Roman coffins in the garden? Well, they're rare: but what was far rarer, were the zinc shells found inside them when they were dug up; and *these* our gardener was allowed to sell for what they would fetch — as zinc!"

They finished in the church, of which the tiles, like the sarcophagi mentioned, were Roman and had been given up by the earth after centuries of jealous hoarding. Camilla was aware of a delicate design on them which she had not noticed before. Also she learnt for the first time what an aumbry was, including the distinction between piscina and lavabo. Constance had been right in her early conjecture that she was not "a good Catholic"; for a good Catholic would have recognised and welcomed these Romish survivals in a church built years before the Reformation; but the wonder to Camilla was how this careless young fellow, with a reputation for unprofitableness which had already reached her, should know so much about such things. When he had made her sit in the squire's pew, her wonder burst out in a question; and Tony, leaning on the doors, with his chin on his folded arms, laughed into her upturned face.

"I'm a fearful fraud, if you only knew," he replied.

"A fraud! What's that?"

"Well, I've been talking about what I don't understand a bit, really. I've been telling you this and that as though I could have told you that and the other if I liked; but in point of fact it's all I know — picked up from two or three people interested in old churches, whom I've shown over this one at odd times."

"So that's being a fraud!"

"Yes. I'm other things too, as you may have heard: the black sheep of the family, for one."

Camilla had an inspiration as to the phrase.

67

"A *mauvais sujet*?"

"*Oui*, mademoiselle — I mean Senhora."

"You know Portuguese, too?"

"Rather! Just enough to call you Senhora Camilla!"

"Then you are very clever; and I shall call you Senhor Antonio. I called you that to the girls, and they laughed."

"They would. It makes me long for a dagger and guitar. I say, though: now I've told you everything about this place, you might tell me something about Portugal."

She gave him a quick, penetrating glance, as if to discover whether he was in earnest. Certainly he was smiling; but if he was not earnest, his smile was very kind and encouraging; and indeed his face seemed the kindest she had seen since saying goodbye to her father — of whom Tony somehow reminded her. She was convinced of his cleverness: for he was the first person who had not spoken of Spain instead of Portugal. She forgot Winnie, furthermore; but then Winnie had never shown any interest in her beloved [country]. Now that she had it, she knew that the question just asked her was what she had been waiting and waiting for the whole week. Tony had put it before talking to her [for] twenty minutes; but then he had himself known her in one minute; and already she seemed to know him as well as she knew Winnie and Constance, and to like him better — because she forgot Winnie.

"Of course I mean it," he said, in answer to her doubting question. "I know your people out there are bigwigs, and that you lived in a fort; that sounds romantic: and I want to know what it was like."

Her eyes sparkled, and a touch of sunlight, flickering between her face and her hair as she moved her head, added to her animated appearance, which Tony duly appreciated over the door. For the squire's pew was not the one in which she had sat and meditated alone; that was in the body of the church, at the other side; and the sunlight playing upon her was part of the very patch which had fascinated him then. This one was west of the pulpit, with walls as high as Tony's shoulders, and [a] fireplace. Camilla's eyes dropped, and fastened on the fireplace, as she answered:

"I would like to describe it to you; but I find so difficult your English language."

"Nonsense! You speak uncommon well. I want to hear about the fort. Your grandfather's at least Duke, isn't he?"

"A count — and a most extraordinary man. He has lived in the fort before I was born. It is near the mouth of the Tagus, at a village on a hill, an hour's drive from Lisbon. It is built on the side of the hill, so although you can stand in the courtyard and peep through the battlements it would kill you to drop down on the other side; but you can look through at the Tagus, which is the bluest water in the world; at least I have seen none like it since I left. I don't know what else I can tell you. The courtyard is full of pepper-trees and seats to sit on; and in the evening we bring out the card-tables and the lamps."

"Ah! You play cards, do you?

"We played every night at home. The Count is very fond of it. I must tell you he is an extraordinary gambler. He has lost one fortune, and would lose another if he had it. He goes in all the lotteries, but never wins, and has papered a room with his unsuccessful coupons!"

"Then I call him a grand old sportsman — that's the true sportsmanlike spirit!" cried Tony. For a moment his face remained comically grave, as he pictured four walls papered with coupons. Then the comic irony of the idea pricked his sense of fun to the quick, and, in spite of the place, he burst into a fit of uncontrollable laughter. Camilla, pleased with herself for pleasing him, added her own peals to his and stopped when he stopped, suddenly — and watched his face as he turned, letting his arms fall from the pew door, and strode down the aisle.

"Stay where you are," said he over his shoulder, in an undertone; "it's the Rector!"

And the Rector it was, pale and stern as usual, but silent. He advanced to the pew without a word, without haste, and without taking immediate notice of his son. He opened the pew-door, and stood behind it, still without speaking. And Camilla made as graceful an exit as she could. Then at last he turned to his son.

Tony, who had not seen his father since his return, was holding out his hand; but Mr Pontifex took no notice of that either.

"It is a pity," said he, more quietly than the young man expected, "that you should choose this place of all others for laughter and — and play. I am waiting for you to lead the way, Anthony."

"My dear father, I found Camilla studying the place alone, and I assisted her studies."

"You were doing so when I came in, I suppose! Pray do not keep me standing here."

"We had fallen into a chat," said Tony, half in exposition, half in play, "and I'm afraid we rather forgot where we were."

"I'm afraid so too. Will you have the goodness to lead the way out?"

Camilla had been trying hard to add a word; but she could not catch the Rector's eye; and the glare he directed at Tony frightened her. She half stopped as she passed the pew on the floor of which the precious beads still reposed; but the

Rector was on her heels; and she had more than his present anger to fear if she turned and told him about them now. She passed the pew resolutely, determining to tell no one, but to return for them after tea.

In the churchyard the Indian file was broken; the Rector returned to the house by the french window of his own study; and as the culprits entered the hall together, Tony remarked:

"We've begun by getting into a row together; but don't think anything more about it. It's me he's angry with, not you; besides, he always says more than he means; and you won't hear another word about this. I'm simply sorry!"

An immediate contradiction came from the study door, which opened at that moment; for thither Tony was sternly summoned.

"I have one thing to say to you," said Mr Pontifex, with his back to the fireplace; "but though you listen to nothing else, you shall listen to this, so that you may be fairly warned. I have given up expecting any good of you. That is why I concern myself no longer with your movements, but we are still thankful to have you amongst us, when you can behave yourself. I still hope, though faintly, that one day you will reform. But meanwhile there is one point on which you must be warned. If you marry without my knowledge and against my will I am done with you; you are not my son — for instance, if you marry an actress, a barmaid, or a Roman Catholic!"

# Chapter VII:  Very Small Talk

Young Pontifex saw no more of his entertaining cousin until the five minutes preceding dinner, when they met in the drawing-room with a mutual stare: for evening dress had transformed and improved them both.  Three independent conversations were already going on, and they managed to snatch a fourth, Camilla signing that she had something to tell him.

"Do you know what I have been doing since tea?" she whispered.

"Well, I heard the bagatelle balls and my father's voice; were you the other player?"

"Yes!"

"How on earth did it happen?"

"I was alone in the hall, and your father came out and found me.  He asked me to play, and we played three games.  I was disappointed, because I wanted to do something else, to go back to the church: I was looking for the key."

"I hope you didn't tell him so.  You are evidently forgiven, but you mustn't go back there — just yet."

"I must!"

"Well, don't let him see you.  I'm glad you played with him.  He's a singular fancy for the rotten game — it's his soft spot — and we hate it.  He beat you, I see: he's having quite a lively chat with Lady Hope, and as a rule they don't have much to say to each other.  I watched them, and looked grave.  How nice the old boy is looking!  I wonder which is the whitest hair, his or hers?"

"There is no difference.  I suppose hers would be the colour of mine?"

"Constance told you that!"

"Yes, she did. I want to ask you! Who is it she is talking to — I didn't catch his name — the other *padre*?"

"The other *what*? I say Camilla, don't come out with that before the Rector!"

"Is it wrong?"

"It smells of Rome. And Rome isn't nice in his nostrils. Not that *I* care, and as for Atkinson — that's his name — he'd rather like it. He's half a Catholic already, Constance tells me; but he plays bagatelle with my father."

"I am a whole one."

"I forgot, but I don't care. *I* am nothing — much. A Pagan, perhaps."

"You are very wicked to say so."

The futile exchange was put an end to by the commencement of dinner. Camilla sailed across the hall on the arm of Erskine Hope; and a better looking couple it would have been difficult to imagine; but the girl was discontented, though the prospect had pleased her before Tony's return. And Tony had returned only that afternoon, and altogether, as yet, Camilla had not spent an hour in his company. This was difficult to realise when she looked round the table and felt she knew him better than any of them — unless it was Winnie; and as she did so, the familiar nod and smile he gave her through the ferns made it more difficult still. She fell to wondering whether she had even yet got to know any other person so quickly before; and a polite remark from Erskine led her to the decision that *he*, at all events, was not the other person.

Yet of this young man she had already seen a good deal. She seemed to have seen him every day. She had not yet been to the Hall, of which, indeed, the girls fought shy, by order. But it appeared to be his habit to turn up at the

73

Rectory most days of the week; his handsome apparition at the schoolroom window neither caused surprise nor entailed the slightest form of greeting; and Camilla observed, what could not fail to strike a foreigner, that she was the only one ever to shake hands with him.  It took her some time to acquire for these occasions the nod and smile [of her cousins], which indeed was familiar almost to contempt, though one of them seemed ever to shine in his company.  As for Camilla, she had not divested herself of formality towards him; but then his attentions, which were not yet as yet marked, were themselves ceremonious.  Camilla found him polite, kind, very obliging, and if not amusing, very ready to be amused — the more popular trait, after all.  She qualified him with a new adjective, one every bit as just as its predecessor (for which she learnt a synonym), and not less offensive: he was now "as nice as he was handsome".  Also, she was not unconscious of a distinction for which she was yet to find a name: he was conspicuously the gentleman.  Tonight she should have found him nicer than ever, for he made a point of talking about Lisbon — a subject which, at other opportunities, Constance had deftly changed — or rather, on hearing him talk, the subject changed.   Others heard her too; though not Constance, who was in animated conversation with her High Church friend, obtaining the most admirable material for amusing comment in the room.

"You have never been to a bull-fight?" Erskine suggested.

"On the contrary," cried Camilla, "I have been to a hundred bull-fights!  That is no exaggeration I am sure.  I think them charming."

"But aren't they rather dreadful?" inquired her companion, who was quite sure she did not mean "charming".

Camilla gave that curious shrug of her shoulders which

74

began at the waist and was traceable to the top of her head. "It is nothing when you are used to it."

"Yet you kill the bulls!!"

"Oh no; we never kill; we have twelve bulls, one after the other, for ten minutes each. They run around one man for the ribbons."

"From the darts! It must hurt them, you know."

Again the shrug; followed by a vivacious account of the bulls' experience with *cavaleiros* and *bandarilheiros*, and her private opinion as to the artistic superiority of the *bandarilheiros*. Yes, there was an accident sometimes; not often. As for the bulls, it could not hurt them, for the same bulls fought over and over again, week after week.

"Saturday after Saturday," exclaimed Erskine, "as a man plays football!"

"No, no! Sunday after Sunday."

Of course the Rector heard it. The girl was on his left, and for some minutes Lady Harriett, on his other hand, had been listening to her, instead of to him. He raised his heavy white eyebrows and frowned very formidably; but for the visitors it is certain that he would have spoken plainly to his niece; and later in the evening, when compelled so to speak, he regretted his previous most unusual self-restraint.

But at present the little dinner-party was going off very well — wonderfully well, considering that there was no wine. That was felt, though it had been anticipated; and it cannot have improved anyone's temper to feel it. To offer water, "and water to add to it", to a tableful of adult guests is to offer them each a tacit but villainous insult. Still, the insult was robbed of some [of] this villainy by the clever management of Constance - who indeed had managed a very pretty table. A water bottle and tumbler was set to every person, and the glass, like the silver, being beautifully clean (trust Constance), and the water good water, there was something chaste and not unattractive in its appearance. With regard to Lady Harriett, who found it difficult to dine without her glass of champagne, it were bold to aver that indigestion as she sat down was not fully compensated by an immeasurable sense of virtue when she got up. A pretty and profound management of flowers had consoled her senses to some extent; the glitter of silver older than her own, and much more highly burnished, also pleased her eyes. The dinner, though simple, had been excellent in its way; and the Rector had made himself unexpectedly polite and conversational. He had talked politics principally, on which they did not, if ever, disagree. Mr Pontifex held turbulent views, shook his hoary old head and prophesied evils to come to the country from the misdemeanours of the laity. He would have hanged a certain statesman side by side with another notoriety who had lately committed a particularly diabolical murder, and his worst prophecy, which concerned the iniquitous growth of education, was very bad indeed: "In ten years' time, Lady Harriett, we shan't be able to get a ploughman! That is what will come of teaching them to read and write!" Lady Harriett did not disagree and appeared to think with him, but the prophecy did not visibly distress her. She rose from the table in the most amiable temper and made a point of congratulating Constance on everything, but particularly on her silver, the secrets of which she desired to know. Constance was delighted, but could not say; Tony whispered "by slaving the slavies" to Winnie, who added "and me, please"; and, for obvious reasons, ladies and gentlemen went back into the drawing-room together.

Mr Atkinson and the hostess took immediate possession of

the piano, where they both sang songs, he in a high tenor, she in a meritorious soprano. He was a cheerful man with a shaven face and the remains of a horque [?], and he rendered his secular love songs with a fervour barely becoming in him: anyone would have said that the pair were in love, save those who knew Constance's opinion of him. She would sing duets with him tonight — their voices harmonised capitally — and tomorrow make profane fun of his cassock and candles, Meanwhile Lady Harriett, who had no patience with her young priest for his absurd attention in that quarter, and had told him so, talked all the time he was singing — to Camilla, who at last she had succeeded in getting to herself.

"Don't *you* sing, my dear?" she asked, gazing fondly at the new idol of her eyes, for whom a niche in her heart also was [al]ready awaiting.

"A little," Camilla said.

"A little! We know what that means. I'm sure you have voices in Spain."

"I have not sung since I arrived in England."

"You shall in a minute," said Lady Harriett; "you may make up your mind to it."

But the minute threatened to be a long one, for Mr Pontifex, disapproving of the prolonged confabulation on the sofa, artfully proposed to Lady Harriett a game of cribbage, which, with whist, was permitted in the Rectory on special occasions. The lady perceived the trap, and refused [to] fall into it, but constructed one herself by a counter-proposal of whist — that was to say, if Camilla played. Camilla did: her uncle was surprised to hear it: but a rubber would keep her out of mischief too, and a pause coming in the music, Mr Pontifex called for volunteers. A hearty chord on the piano was the answer from that quarter, but Tony good-naturedly came forward; and the table was being arranged when Camilla rose from her seat in slight confusion.

"I have not got my purse," said she.

"You won't want it my dear," interposed Lady Harriett in a hasty undertone; but Mr Pontifex had heard, and turned round to exclaim "Want what?"

"My purse."

The Rector surveyed her with undisguised severity.

"What do you want with your purse?"

"For — for the game," said Camilla, as boldly as she could; but she felt her ground crumble under her notwithstanding.

Mr Pontifex stared at her until her eyes fell, and the colour mounted to her face, and concentrated in two red spots, a rose-leaf on either cheek.  Then he turned to Lady Harriett Hope.

"If you do not mind, Lady Harriett," he said, taking the two packs of cards from the table as he spoke, and placing them in his tail-coat pockets, "we will forgo our rubber of whist.  We will not play cards at all.  My niece is evidently accustomed to play for money.  As  I do not approve of that, we will from tonight give up the practice of card-playing in this home.  We shall not miss it.  We do not play more than once or twice in the year.  Moreover, now I speak of it, I lately made up my mind to this effect.  I had forgotten."

He glanced at Tony, who was gazing at the carpet, and grinding it with his heels.  Lady Harriett's indignation was scarcely less.

"Of course she's accustomed to play for money," she cried, patting Camilla's hand; "it is the custom of her country.  You have been used to what you couldn't help, haven't you my dear?  In Turkey you must do what the Turkeys do, you know, Mr Pontifex — likewise in Spain!"

The laugh with which the old lady's brilliance was received cleared the atmosphere at a needed moment, but she had not finished.

"Personally, Mr Pontifex, I am only too glad not to play. I want to hear your niece sing."

"She does sing," said Mr Pontifex, who, to do him justice, was half sorry for what he had said, now that he had said it; "your father told me you did. Are your songs down here?"

They were not; they were in her room; she had never brought them down. She went for them now most willingly; and Tony held the door open, and whispered an encouraging "Cheer up!" as she passed. He thought her shoulders quivered at his words; but that was the only sign she gave that she was not altogether lacking emotions, and only Tony saw it.

"I wonder you have never asked [her] to sing before," said Mr Pontifex to Constance; he was not used to repeating his words, and the new experience was amazing; but Constance replied that she had never thought of it, as she put away her own music and beat a rather ostentatious retreat from the piano; and felt annoyed with Mr Atkinson because he did not follow her but sat on the music stool waiting to be of use.

Camilla took some time in fetching her music. When she returned, with a stout portfolio under her arm, the rose-leaves still lay on either cheek. She blushed as prettily as she cried: but no one saw her cry: and only one person suspected that she had been doing so now.

Half a minute later [she] was sitting on the music stool, with the lighted candles shining softly on her plain white dress and rich, heightened colour, and playing rather nervously the prefatory bass of her song. Tall Mr Atkinson bent over her to turn over the leaves, thus exciting in the heart of Constance an irritation which the quality of the new voice was calculated to increase. It proved to be a soprano of surprising compass, with magnificent lower notes, clear high ones, and of a timbre which gained unconsciously from the young girl's nervousness. It was a voice which might make a fortune, if necessary, in after years; already the girl had been well taught, and she sang with her whole heart; but at present her fault was loudness — which also was accentuated, just now, by her nervousness. But it was a fault not generally noticed. The song fairly thrilled the company, though they did not understand the words, which were in Italian. The emotional Lady Harriett shed tears, and even Mr Pontifex beat time with his finger. He never did so when Constance sang.

The praise and applause when the song was over was a little overwhelming; it eliminated the blushes, and brought them back swiftly; and red as their owner Mr Atkinson was ill-advised to go over to Constance and whisper:

"She *can* sing, can't she? You and I had better give it up — I never heard anything like it."

"Didn't you?" said Constance. "She has a powerful voice, certainly; but if I were you I should suggest the sordine to her, while you *are* there."

"The sordine?"

"The sordine: look it up in a dictionary."

The other listener who refrained from saying anything which might turn Camilla's head was Mr Pontifex. Nevertheless he was the first to ask her to sing again; and in her second song, a simple French one, Camilla was altogether lighter and more charming. The Rector beat time once more with his fingers, but again refrained from actual applause; and Lady Harriett essayed a fresh flow of tears, all to herself. She was enchanted, and did not hide her enchantment. She kissed the singer effectively on each rose-leaf — they were still there

— when she said goodbye, and made her promise to come to the Hall and sing to her for a whole afternoon. "Until you are hoarse! And then," whispered the wicked old woman, "we will play cards — for our last penny! So bring your purse."

And Erskine, who stood by beaming, added a more vigorous pressure of the hand than was either warranted by the occasion or actively consistent with the character of gentlemanly reserve.

# Chapter VIII:  Wilful Folly

Singing, unfortunately, was a weak as well as a strong point of Constance Pontifex: she sang very nicely indeed, but not so nicely as she thought she sang.  Still, even Constance was capable of recognising a superiority about which there could be no question; and in Camilla's voice she acknowledged a calibre to which her own could not pretend; but the acknowledgment was made only to herself — not to Winnie, certainly, who gave indiscreet expression to her enthusiasm as the girls were going to bed.  Constance sneered at her through the open door between their adjoining rooms, and instantly regretted her sneer, because it might sound as if she were jealous.  As if she could descend to jealousy — of the Portuguese!  But Winnie was idiot enough to imagine anything, and to prevent misconception Constance gave her a cold goodnight and closed the door between them.  Alone she allowed herself to become thoroughly annoyed — at the idea of Winnie's misjudging her, she fancied.  It is hard to believe that the subject-matter of her annoyance stood aside in her mind for the respectable period she spent on her knees; but at all costs she did not go to sleep over her devotions.  Nor did her conscience allow her to "cut" that Chapter in bed with which this good girl sanctified the close of each day, just because she did not happen to be "in the humour"; she read every verse of it; and her conscience, which was not indulgent after all, allowed her to sip her final literary night-cap from a Work of Fiction.

It was, we may be entirely sure, a very blameless book; but even so it was a Novel, and that on the queer side of Holy Writ, certainly; and it would not have been heard here but for its improving effect on the young lady's temper.  The clownish suggestion of Mr Atkinson — made in fun, of course, but nevertheless in bad taste — that he and she should now give up singing, continued to rankle; and that clergyman's better side vaguely stamped the hero of her story. She forgot Winnie, and the injustice of which her weak mind was capable. She had forgotten Camilla and her disgustingly good voice; when a tap came at her door, and a moment later Camilla herself was in the room — dressed just as she had been dressed all the evening.

"*Why* haven't you gone to bed?" asked Constance, leaving a finger in her book as she closed it in her amazement.

Camilla came close to the bed. "I — I am unhappy!" She looked perplexed.

"What in the world about?"

"I — I can hardly tell you!"

"Then why have you come?"

The questions were unsympathetic, certainly, and most unsympathetically put: but Camilla could not perceive the point of the last one, and it forced her to be explicit.

"It is about my necklace — You remember the necklace I told you I wore always?"

"I remember it. I noticed you hadn't it on tonight, and I hoped you had given up always wearing it after what I said."

"No," said Camilla sadly; "that is not the case. It came to pieces in the old church this afternoon."

And she briefly described the accident, and why she had not brought the beads away with her — although she knew exactly where they were, in the third pew from the end — and how she had been prevented from going back for them. How also, in the excitement of singing, she had [momentarily] forgotten [them].

"It is a pity to let that sort of thing excite you," Constance took the opportunity of saying. "This comes of superstition, you see; I don't wonder at your being ashamed to tell them; but what's the use of bothering about it now?"

Camilla twisted a tiny laced pocket-handkerchief between her white fingers.

"Well?" said Constance.

"I want my beads."

"I am afraid you will have to want them."

"I have never been without them since they were fastened on, when I was quite a little girl. I dare not go to bed without them."

Constance reopened her book. "You had better wake the Rector and tell *him* so." She read a paragraph and then looked up. Camilla was gazing wistfully at Winnie's door. "Winnie will be asleep," said Constance, divining her thought; "and so ought you to be." And to show an example she shut up her book, laid it on the table, and fingered her extinguisher. "I also am going to sleep."

"Then I leave you."

Something in the tone gave Constance a twinge.

"My dear Camilla, I am really sorry about it, much as I hate superstition," said she, speaking kindly for the first time; "but what can I do? You would not have me jump out of bed and run over to the church with you *now* — at midnight?"

One of Camilla's gloomy [sighs] prefaced her humble answer: "No; I see it is impossible. It was very absurd of me. Goodnight, Constance." And she was gone.

But, as some persons are too utterly amiable to see an insult at the time, and resent it all the more when they do see it on reflection, so Camilla became very angry indeed when once more in her own room, and alone. So far her anger was like her tears — none had seen it yet, in England — and this

84

was another aesthetic shame. She gave way to very pretty anger tonight, in her own room. Constance had been cruel and cutting to her; the cuts she had not felt at the time, but they hurt all the more for that now. If she had merely refused to help her to recover her precious amulet tonight, this girl would have forsaken, though sadly, a notion which she knew in her heart to be wild and ridiculous. But the manifestly ridiculous stands most in need of the least ridicule; too much has the effect of the double negative, and it ceases to seem ridiculous; and Camilla, though she had called her idea absurd — as indeed it was — in order to close a futile appeal, saw it now in anything but the absurd light which with kindness and sympathy she would not have denied. On the other hand, her mind flew through the closed door of Winnie's room: Winnie would not have refused her: Winnie would have stolen out with her — down the back-stairs and out by the schoolroom door, rather enjoying the adventure — and in five minutes they would have been in their rooms, with beating hearts perhaps, but with those amber beads. She had a new thread ready for them. She would have lain down, safe and happy, with the dear beads once more coolly pressing her neck.

She could not lie down as it was; at any rate, she would not. She sat on the corner of her bed, her folded arms heaving, her dark eyes flashing, and every drop of southern blood tingling in her veins. With all her sweetness, she was an only child, and in Portugal, in the strong sunshine and deep shadows of the ancient, she had been indulged by everyone, from the soft-hearted, grumbling old Count, her grandfather, to black Delphine the cook. One and all had given her her own way when she wanted it. She had not wanted it often, her nature being singularly free from selfishness, though not from wilfulness, which is another thing. But she did want her way tonight — even more than her necklace — though the superstitious importance she attached to the wearing of that bauble should not be exaggerated. And what Constance had said, with her manner of saying it, concentrated that wilfulness from which she was not free, and rolled it in her soul, a fiery ball, tightening the nerves and stupefying common-sense.

How good it would be to get the beads for herself — now — and to wake Constance, if she required waking in five minutes — that was all it would take — to show them to her, careless of the consequences! How good; and how easy! Mr Pontifex, under the softening influence of bagatelle, had restored the church key to its nail in the hall. Camilla had audaciously carried it upstairs with her. It was in her pocket now. She felt its weight. And she would find her beads again — in the third pew from the end.

While making up her mind to go to Constance — who knew about the necklace — Camilla had sat at her open window. It was open still, and she went back to it now. She sat down again, in the chair there, leant her elbow on the sill, and fixed her eyes on the old church. It stood but a matter of fifty yards from the house. The full moon hung over its thatched roof, the outline of which was broken by the gently-waving tops of the elm trees — whether on this or that side of the church it was impossible to say. For the moon was on that side; church and trees and the clear sky with sharpened lines filled in with ink; and so very slight was the movement of branches that their whisper scarcely touched her ear at the open window. Nor did the night air chill her: the night was soft, the air warm. And below her window was the schoolroom, with its own garden-door; and outside her door the back-stairs leading down to it.

She was not without natural tremors and terrors of the night; she wished to have done this thing rather than to do it; and her desire at least she had given up combating since her return from Constance. She had already gone through the performance in her mind, and revelled in its imaginary achievement; and this is a normal stage of temptation. The opportunity was present and even pressing. Fear was the only hindrance; but fear never yet triumphed over opportunity and desire, in a nature not free from wilfulness. Camilla had only her abler self to conquer; and conquer it she did, by degrees.

Five minutes only: that time would be ample. She held her watch in her hand for that space, and considered herself outside the schoolroom door on the grass — half a minute. Her eye travelled to the churchyard gate — half a minute. It picked its way among the shadows — half a minute — to the promontory side by the tower, which she must double to get at the door on the far side. So her eye rested on the tower for two whole minutes — short measure, perhaps, for the unlocking of the church door and all that was to be done inside. Another minute and a half and she was back in her room, breathless but triumphant.

She sprang to her feet. If she had done all this not merely with her eyes! She *would* do it.

The cuckoo in the hall struck the half-hour as she opened her bedroom door, a shawl round her shoulders and a pair of tennis shoes lent her by Winnie (some sizes too large for her) on her feet; otherwise [she was attired] as she had been all the evening. It was half past twelve. She heard the clock ticking in the hall; but she was not going to the hall. (She heard also sonorous music of which she inclined to suspect her uncle.) She crept down the steep stairs at hand; they had no comforts; they creaked, and she lost a minute in waiting to be found out.  She nearly turned back; but that was not a thing she was in the habit of doing; her nerves, too, were still taut, and the feel of the school-room door handle gave her fresh courage.  As she advanced the moonlight glinted on her through the shutters.  That further encouraged her, and very soon was where she had first pictured herself from her window; but not in a minute and half; already she had taken twice that time.  However, to fly over the dewy grass was simple work; she gained the church-yard gate in quick time.

Her heart beat, not from breathlessness only, as she undid the latch and opened the gate.  The shadow of the church stretched almost to the fence: she stood already in that of the tower; in front of her was no gravel path, but an ill-refined gray track, twisting among the fallen mounds and gray, tilted stones of the old churchyard.  Her feet were already wet through with the heavy dew. In the shadow of the church, the graves frightened her.  But she would not turn back.  In five more minutes — in much less than five now — she would be back in her room with her beloved beads; she fortified herself by recalling her triumphant sensation, and also by glancing back at the window of her room, where she had left the candle burning.

Pushing on, however, while looking over her shoulder, she was suddenly brought to her knees on a grave: but sprang to her feet with a sharp cry and an involuntary one, for a light shone on her face from the church windows.  It was the moon shining through the windows of the opposite side; but a horrible moment passed before she realised this: that moment had made her throb; with a desperate rush she darted to the tower, and paused, fainting, only in the porch.

But now the moon shone full upon her; she could see the shaking of her hands as she fitted the key into its hole, and the cold touch of it accentuated the reactionary chill setting in within her veins. Three from the end — three from the end — and in less time than it had taken her to come she would be back in her room. The key grated loudly on the silent night, the door swung open obedient to her push, she dived in and stood motionless — stilled by the rigidity of the scene.

The moon shone through the windows in solid shafts of pale light, beneath one of which stood Camilla, as under a ladder. The light fell on wooden benches, stone pillars, red tiles, turning all to an ashen gray; beyond lay the chancel, bathed in a bluish haze; above the roof was a starless sky. A moonbeam touched the font and reached over it to the lack-leg [?] ladder of the little corner gallery.

A mouldy, airless smell, not noticeable in daytime, struck Camilla's nostrils. She stood transfixed, as in the halls of death, the scent and stillness of it oppressing her soul. A flutter of wings in the belfry aided the moonlight in reminding her exactly where she was. She gathered fresh courage — the concentration of all that remained to her — and panted up the aisle. Three from the end! She dragged open the door, and dropped upon hands and knees: no beads fell upon her hands. She swept them in widening circles, but no beads settled rattled from them against the sides of the pew: then she raised and wrung them — for the beads were her mother's!

She knelt motionless, in a newer, vaguer terror. Three from the end? Had she made a mistake? She rose at the thought; she was in the aisle, with her hand on the rear of another pew; yet instead of opening it — instead of turning back — she suddenly flew through the blue haze of the chancel, fell on her knees as she did stop before the wooden relic of the altar, and raised her head in prayer. As in the afternoon, a step had sounded in the porch, and was now approaching up the flagged aisle. As it came nearer she pressed her fingers in her ears, and her lips moved.

"Nassa Senhor," she began in broken tones, " — " [*At this point in the manuscript Camilla is literally lost for words, for the author has left himself a space of two or three lines in which to insert some Portuguese utterances.*]

"Camilla," said a voice above her, loud enough to be heard through her thumbs, "are you walking in your sleep?"

She turned with a joy that stopped her hand: for once more the steps had been those of Tony Pontifex.

"My dear girl, what on earth have you been doing? Thank Heaven I had not gone to bed. I sit up smoking hard and was in time to see you passing my window. There, don't cry; you *have* been walking in your sleep!"

He slipped a hand under each of her arms and raised her gently. Then, supporting her in the hollow of his strong right arm, he led her, shaking with sobs, down the aisle and out into the charmed moonlight. There he released her, dipped his hands into the wet grass, and held them to her throbbing temples; and then he made her sit on a flat stone until she was recovered, standing over her in simple kindness.

"Oh, Tony" she murmured at last, through her tears.

"Well? Do you feel able to walk to the house?"

"Yes" — with a sigh.

"I do not want you to waken them."

"You will not tell them?"

"No."

"Is it possible? Oh, thank you — thank you!"

"Come, it's nothing to cry about; yet I ought to wake somebody if you don't feel fit, you know!"

"I am all right."

"And if you often did it?"

"I never did it before."

"Well, come then. Here's my arm. I know how you got out, we'll get in the same way."

And Camilla did; but Tony waited below on the path until he saw her at her window, looking very white and spectral in the moonlight as she softly lowered the sash, and then the blind. He waited much longer, doubting his wisdom in not waking anybody, and deciding that the reason nobody woke of his or her own accord was simply his wish lest another would do so. He waited even after the light was out, little dreaming that she was crying afresh on her pillow — partly from normal and well-merited effects of her fright, partly at his kindness, and partly for her beads, which she had not recovered after all; and it seemed to her superstitious mind — and to her susceptible heart proper — that the bad omen which she believed it to be bore direct reference to the new friendship which a single day had made and welded.

But Tony went back to lock up the church — and slapped his thigh with the key the moment he had done so.

"If this is sleepwalking," he thought, "it's the rummiest one I've ever had to deal with or read [about]. But she *is* a rum 'un altogether — a rum 'un right through!" — which was hardly [the] way Camilla was thinking of him.

# Chapter IX: Upstairs and Downstairs

His doubts as to the genuine somnambulistic character of the late moonlight prank, though in some ways a relief, perplexed and worried the good-natured Tony more than he realised; he was, in fact, strongly tempted to divulge the incident to the private ear of his young sister, whose tried closeness might certainly have excused the breakage of his word; but he was glad he had not broken it (and to be able to say so) when, next forenoon, Camilla came to him and of her own accord made a clean breast of the whole affair. She told him everything, down to the history and superstitious significance of her blessed beads; and, tilting her chin, she brought two of these to light, her finger-tip dividing them and showing the new cord. She had recovered them all after breakfast in the third pew from the *far* end — and this time had skimmed back to her room on wings, there and then to thread and re-fasten them beyond the possibility of fresh disaster. So now she was happy, though paler than usual, and not without secret apprehensions of necessary evils to come.

Tony raised his glance from the shining amber and spheres to the darker brilliance of her eyes, and his own showed an open admiration which her various attractions had not hitherto produced in him.

"Upon my soul, I never dreamt you were such a determined young woman! I wouldn't have thought it of you. I like your pluck, though, by Jove I do!"

Camilla responded with a sceptical shake of her head: "It is very kind of you to say so — but it is impossible. You think me very foolish. You do not believe in luck!"

"Don't I?" chuckled Tony. "That's rather good, that is — seeing that if there's one thing I *do* believe in, it's luck! As to that, it's about the only thing I don't jolly well disbelieve in; and I know something about it; I've had good and bad. Last year I backed the winner of the Leger for every cent I could raise; *that* was the biggest bit of luck man ever had; but you wouldn't understand if I was to tell you."

"I am afraid you are as bad as my grandfather, who will not stir an inch in his chair when he is winning — no matter how uncomfortable he becomes — for fear of changing his luck!" laughed Camilla, irreverently. "He is an extraordinary man. I am not as bad as that. And I *was* foolish, and am very sorry about it, whatever you say; for the worse is, it was wrong."

"Not so very, now, come! Where was the harm? The worst thing you did, though, was to go to Constance. Let me recommend Winnie to you in a case of that kind — in most cases, indeed, except one of illness. Constance has her points: go to her if you've an ache or a pain that she can put her finger on, and she'll take care of you: she's at her best when you're really bad, though you've got to do what she tells you. But don't go to her in a bother. Go to Winnie: she hasn't got the head and hands; but she has everything else."

"Certainly there is a great difference between them."

"You're right; though as I tell you, old Constance has her points. But Winnie's the girl for my money, I must own. Have you noticed how everybody calls her Winnie? Now Constance was never Connie in her life; and there you have your difference between 'em in a nutshell."

"They are both very kind to me," said Camilla, simply; "so are you all."

He took off his straw-hat to her.

"But take my tip, Camilla: you hang on to Winnie. She's the temperate one. The Rector and Constance are at the extreme end of the morals and religions plank — and I daresay they'd tell you I more than balance them at the other!"

His meaning was divined rather than understood. He meant that his character was reputed not good in the family. It might be true, too: but he did not look bad: he had not the look of certain truly shocking characters with whom she had played cards in her grandfather's courtyard; though even they had not shocked her with an exhibition of the cloven hoof. The mere knowledge of its existence had not horrified her — in those gentlemen — as it would have horrified Winnie, for instance. She had been brought up differently, as few English girls are brought up, with lantern flashes into the murky corners of life; yet Winnie's heart was not more honest — thanks to that constitutional shrug!   Camilla's shrug was unconsciously her defiant weapon: the blade that cut down Care and still blacker jockeys of the spirit: her Excalibur.

Tony's character was a privileged rider: it was allowed to stick on. He was not as those notorious gentlemen of Portugal, who had shown her superficial kindness, of a sort. He, in a few hours, had shown her kindness of another sort which she had taken, no doubt, too gratefully to heart.   Whatever he said about Winnie, she looked upon himself already as her best friend, she could not help it, and there was an excuse — he had been her friend in need.  It troubled her to imagine her friend the *mauvais sujet* he was made out, not only by his own hints, but by remarks that had passed before his return.  The thought that he might be bad under all his kindness — bad as it was her misfortune to wot of badness — came to her against her will, and turned Excalibur's edge.  So much for letting one jockey perch.

It was when the family were gathered together, at the table, that she felt him peculiarly her friend.  The average meal at the Rectory was a business, with economy of language for its principle, and the silence alone had made it an ordeal to Camilla (who was used to something very different) before Tony's return.   His cheerful presence at once ameliorated the depressing daily scenes.   Not that he forced the conversation: but because Camilla had only to catch his eye to feel the warmth and light of his jolly, reassuring smile.   Nor was he only firm across the table: today she could not eat — was not hungry, and was also unaccustomed to midday meals: and it was Tony who did all the foreseeing, and at last induced her to swallow some morsels, long after Constance had tacitly abandoned her as "stubborn".   And after luncheon his solicitude took a more particular, though embarrassing, shape.

He inveigled her upstairs, on the pretext of showing her his sanctum under the tiles.   And he did show her what this was — a scratch team of pipes, tobacco-jars, ashes in a soup-plate, sporting and theatrical prints (of which he had twice that show at Cambridge, he observed), and an untidy stack of newspapers, of a uniformly florid complexion, and the view from the window.   But these were quickly inspected, and evidently he had some other object in bringing her upstairs.

"Sit down there," he said, pointing to the armchair; "it's your friend Felix's place, but I'm delighted to find him from home. He sleeps his brain to a pulp, that dog. Sit down there — and hold on."

Camilla had obliged him — to an extent.   She had taken a light seat on the arm of the chair, and was rather curiously watching her cousin, who had turned his back to her as he talked, and was leaning over an open box.   Presently he rose and faced her, with two wine-glasses in one hand and a bottle in the other. Camilla rose too.

"What do you mean, Tony?"

He set the glasses on the chimney-piece, and filled them,

smiling. "I mean you to have what you're accustomed to; that's all. You're accustomed to wine in your own country, and this is your country's wine; it's choice old port! Come on. You're looking pale. It's the very thing you want."

He took both glasses in his hands and offered her one: she would not take it.

"What's the matter?"

"I do not want it."

"I don't believe you. You used to take it out there at meals?"

"Yes, certainly."

"Well, we've barely finished lunch, and it's your country's wine. You like it, don't you?"

"Oh, yes."

"And it's good for you; so where's the harm?"

She found it difficult to say; for it is difficult to defend lucidly a mere instinct, even in one's own tongue. Her eyes were on the point of her right foot, which was describing little circles upon the pivot of the heel. Those rose-leaves bloomed below them on her cheeks.

"Your father" — she fluttered at length.

He cut her short. His father, she must know, if she had not discovered it already, was in some things a fanatic: an anachronism too. Who but he, at this time of day, would keep no wine in the house and have none upon the table at a dinner-party? It was no good going by the Rector in all his ideas. Either there was harm in drinking a glass of wine, or no harm; in any case it was what Camilla was used to, and it would do her good; and this was the only reason it had entered his head.

She could not argue with him, and her shrug seemed to settle the matter; she took the glass from him, too, and he clinked his against it; but she did not raise her eyes until the rim was on her lips, and just as Tony had emptied his glass; and then her lips never touched the rim at all. She quietly replaced her glass on the chimney-piece, and looked Tony full in the eyes.

"I do not want it! I am very sorry. I am afraid you are very angry with me."

"Not a bit," answered Tony, seeing that she was final, and catching her shrug; "but it needn't be wasted." And he took her untouched glass and himself tossed off the wine without more ado. Then the machinery of a scene which had strangely jarred Camilla was put away; the matter was dismissed; and the young girl affected a piety she did not feel — imagining that she had given him offence, but that he was too kind-hearted to show it. The kindness of his heart was indeed more apparent to her than ever. It hurt her to think she must have hurt him, by refusing what was obviously well-meant, and also quite harmless in her eyes. She hardly knew why she had been so obstinate; but she was sure that she should be obstinate again, in similar circumstances; and equally sure that the circumstances would not recur. She was vexed with herself for having accepted his invitation to the sanctum upstairs; and meanwhile she was for the first time thankful to escape from his company.

Her appreciation of his goodness to her contrasted with her vague resentment of the latest form his goodness had taken. This bothered her, though not, certainly, acutely. It was not a large matter, after all, and it took a really large matter to worry her very much. She had the invaluable armour of a slight natural indifference [, or] so it seemed: but wherever Tony thrust there appeared to be a joint in it, notwithstanding. And she had known him but twenty-four hours.

This consideration in a great measure accounted for the very little he saw of her during the next twenty-four hours. To be

97

just, he did not try hard to see more. When it struck him, a few days later, that he knew her no better than after the first day, the reflection did not depress him. Their friendship was at a standstill: he regarded it as standing still to get breath: for he owned to some pace at starting, though not to having made the pace. It was due to circumstances; and he was not altogether grateful to the circumstances; for Tony Pontifex, if poor on the positive virtues, had at least one negative merit. He was not a male flirt. He held that thing in virile and unaffected contempt. So any idea of nonsense between himself and his pretty slip of a foreign cousin, even if it came into his head, which was unlikely, was the last thing in the world to lodge there.

And the cousin's head, though not so hard, and some five years younger, was quite as incapable of admitting knowingly that kind of nonsense. Nor could she feel in the least danger of doing so at present. Her feeling was very different. But she did feel cheapened in the eyes of Tony; and no feeling is a stronger wedge between woman and man. Moreover, it was he who had first made her feel it — a fact which hammered in the wedge pretty tight. Nevertheless she wrote very kindly about him to her father, who was liable to sail at any time, and more cheerfully than before of her own prospect of a year at Essingham.

# Chapter X: "In my lady's parlour"

So matters stood for some days; and really, all things considered, they might have stood much worse. Starting afresh from their first meeting in the church, matters might easily have stood very much worse indeed, even in these early days: had Tony been an emasculate male flirt, for instance, and Camilla much more of a fool than she really was. Meanwhile she was not too proud to profit by a bit of advice of his. She "hung on" to Winnie, and found her reward in that good girl's selfless devotion and unvarying sweetness of temper. They became so inseparable, and all at once, that certain sneers at their joint expense were not altogether unmerited. They walked by day and talked both day and night; it was a little ridiculous to see them, and Constance prophesied, with seeming safety, that "it would not last"; but this was under the irritation of a Saturday afternoon she found they were spending at the Hall together, without having breathed beforehand a word of their arrangements to anybody.

The fact was, however, that they had made no arrangements of which to breathe. The real culprit was Lady Harriett Hope, from whom, indeed, came the word that the young ladies were at the Hall — she had rescued them from the rain — and would keep them, if she might, until evening. This message, arriving as the others were sitting down to lunch, made Mr Pontifex extremely angry; but the rain, which had been intermittent all the morning, was now falling heavily; and word was ultimately returned, with the girls' waterproofs and Camilla's songs — without which the messenger had orders not to return — that they might stay as long as Lady Harriett cared to keep them, providing they were back to supper.

But the messenger was made to wait; for Constance was not the one to leave the table, even if her father would have allowed it, to hunt for Camilla's songs; so lunch was over at the Hall too when those were handed to Lady Harriett, in the drawing-room. That lady had arranged herself very comfortably in her favourite old armchair, with Camilla gathered close to her side, in front of a welcome fire; Erskine stood with his back to it, in flannels and a blazer; and Winnie watched them from the shadows beyond its rays. Outside the rain was falling in a steady torrent, swishing through the leaves, splashing from the gravel paths, and falling flat, by comparison, on the softened lawns. Erskine was thankful that a match had fallen through; and not only on account of the weather.

"I never remember the names of French songs," remarked Lady Harriett, looking through them, "much less of Spanish. How I wish you sang the old English songs, my dear! But I suppose the pronunciation would be a difficulty, in singing. Not that it matters, though, what you sing; it's your voice we want to hear. Your voice could mean a fortune to some poor girls who haven't a penny, and you have no need of it! Well, you shan't injure it by singing immediately after lunch." The old lady lay back with the songs in her lap. "You shall go on talking about Spain — and that delightful Duke."

"Count," corrected Erskine.

"He is my grandfather," remarked Camilla, not by way of information, but rather as an involuntary confession of doubt as to the seemliness of exposing his amusing eccentricities.

"Then give us some more tales of your grandfather," chuckled Lady Harriett; "he is a man after my own heart!"

Camilla reflected, unable to resist the pleasure of pleasing:

100

and she was beginning to perceive that the least thing concerning that poor old gentleman was quite certain to delight Lady Harriett, for one, among others.

"Oh!" she exclaimed presently, laughing to herself. "I know what to tell you! You know, he has spent one fortune, and wants to spend another if he had it; but now he has only what the Countess gives him, besides his pension. So he very seldom plays at the Fort, but watches us playing, and keeps his money for the few months they spend in the winter at his wife's house in Leesbon — she is not my grandmother, she is his third wife. And she will not allow him to lose; so she has a hole through ceiling, and when he is losing she knocks for him to go to bed!"

The picture did not fail to make them laugh.

"I seem to see them," said Lady Harriett; "yet, you haven't told me what he looks like, nor how he dresses."

"He numbers his clothes!" exclaimed Camilla, her irrelevancy being due to a fresh eccentricity just remembered.

"I'm sorry to hear it — so many people do," observed the old lady drily; "but perhaps his is a special system?"

"I mean that he numbers everything — his socks, and so on — one, two, three, four; he will only wear them in the proper order; and he insists to have the same number all over the body. You do not understand me. Nothing could make him wear number-one collar with number-two socks! He is very angry when his clothes are put out for him with the wrong numbers; he suspects always that Ignacio is stealing them."

"I recommend the plan to you, Erskine," laughed his mother; but that young fellow was most interested in Ignacio, whose name was new. Who was he?

"Cousin to the Countess," answered Camilla; "he lives at the Fort."

"A second — your grandfather?"

"On the contrary; he is a young man like — "

"Like *you*, Erskine," Lady Harriett added for Camilla, who was not yet at ease with "her pretty man", and who was peculiarly on her guard, just now, against lapses into familiarity with young Englishmen. And this one was young enough to connect the slight and momentary blush with the person mentioned, and to remember the name of Ignacio, not with humour, from that day forth.

It was Erskine who at length opened the piano and took Camilla away from his mother. The girl at once got up, at a nod from the old lady. But she hesitated on the hearthrug. There was, in fact, a slight weight on her mind: her singing had nothing to do with it: it had accumulated since a change in the conversation, which had drifted from Lisbon to Essingham: and she now made an effort to remove it, in her own way.

"I don't know what you will think of me, Lady Harriett, for the extraordinary things I have told you about the Count. He is my grandfather — and I think I am horrid! But I haven't told you how kind he is always to me; I *couldn't* tell you; but I assure you, I love him very much."

"My dear child," said Lady Harriett, quite touched by the girl, "you have made him out the most delightful person I ever heard of in my life. I only hope he'll live to win one of those lotteries — and that I may live to see him, some day, when he comes over to see *you*! I don't suppose he'd mind one scrap what you've said. I should say he is just as fond of you as you are of him."

Erskine was inclined to think so, too, as the young girl came over to the piano, bearing on her charming face the warm glow of the fire into the grey light of the rainy afternoon. He stood behind her, with his back to the window, as she sang, and turned over the leaves intelligently — which argued music in his own soul. He had, indeed, himself some idea of singing; but there his reserve came in; he preferred listening — even, say, to Constance.

Lady Harriett folded her white plump hands, and closed her eyes to listen. She could not understand a word — not many words, at all events — she was a high born, but not at all an educated woman, as the age is educated. Her "nieces" had always spoken the necessary French on the Continent; that was why she was not going abroad this year. But if she owned to poverty in the accomplishments, she confessed as frankly to plenitude in the emotions; she was far too sensational; and the thrilling lower notes of Camilla's fine voice touched her to tears as surely as a titillation of the windpipe. The songs were perfectly cheerful, for all she knew; but the very first one made her cry; but it is to be feared that she enjoyed it (at least) no less for that.

She had, however, another favourite sensation: that of proximity to the young of her own sex. Camilla was singing. Where was Winnie?

"Here I am," said a pleasant voice from the dark.

"I'd forgotten you were here!" So had they all. "Come and sit beside me."

Winnie came. Her hair was bonnier in the firelight than Camilla's.

"Why have you been so quiet, my dear?"

"I was listening," laughed Winnie.

"What did you think of the song? Don't answer! Here's another."

And though she knew it, and though it gave constant occasion for Camilla's finest notes (being, in fact, the 'Jewel Song' in Gonoud's *Faust*), this one failed to moisten Lady

Harriett's eyes: for they were inquisitively fixed upon Winnie: who was gazing at what was visible of Erskine, sliced across the chest by the music over which he bent, and behind his head a sky of tarnished silver. As the song ended Winnie turned her head, and knew that she had been watched.

"I believe it has stopped raining," she had the presence of mind to say; "the sky is so much brighter."

"Ah, I saw you looking at the sky," answered Lady Harriett; "and now I suppose you will want to run away and leave us. No? Well, I'm glad; but you're an awful girl for the open air, we know."

Camilla sang to them until tea was brought in. Sunshine followed the tea: a shaft pierced cruelly to the dying fire, and killed it quite. And the charm of the afternoon — the rare charm of the fireside in summer — was over.

The girls picked their way home through the puddles with linked arms. Their heads, too, were close together.

"How did you like it, Camilla?"

"Oh, I liked it immensely. It was a delightful afternoon. But I never knew you so quiet, Winnie. Didn't *you* like it?"

"Of course I did. But I'm best at listening, you know — unless it's with you. Tell me, what do you think of Lady Harriett, now you know her pretty well?"

"I am very fond of her. She is so kind!"

"And Erskine?"

"He is charming."

"But don't you like him too?"

"One cannot help liking him"

"So most people find," observed Winnie, in a tone that meant nothing at all; and she seemed to have no more to say.

"There!" cried Camilla, as they came in silence to the Rectory gate; "you're just like you were at the Hall. I wish I knew what was bothering you — *Winniesinha!*"

Winnie laughed., "*Winniezenyer!* Whatever does it mean?"

"It means — what you would say 'Winnie darling'."

Winnie hugged her arm. "I'm afraid you're a little humbug," she whispered tenderly; but the words were barely uttered, when, with a startled cry, Camilla freed herself and darted up the drive. Winnie gaped. A big man with a red beard was standing on the steps, and into his outstretched arms Camilla rushed headlong.

# Chapter XI: *Untitled*

The big gentleman, into whose arms Camilla had practically flung herself, was, of course, only her father — a person of impulse, like Tony, who rather resembled him in other respects as well. Mr James's latest impulse, moreover, was like many of his nephew's in lying very open to unkind adjectives. He had really played a very inconsiderate trick. His room had been ready for him at the Rectory for some days, because he had warned them to expect him at a few hours' notice; and after all he had omitted to write, and even to wire before leaving town. Nor had he any excuse: he had played the boyish trick of taking people by surprise, and it was hardly to be expected that all the people should appreciate the surprise as highly as Camilla, whose childlike delight was a pretty and rather moving sight. Happily, however, the Rector was not personally inconvenienced. He had looked forward, with private keenness, to his brother's visit; the surprise was entirely pleasant to him, and his welcome was if anything perhaps the warmer for want of preparation. As for Tony, he saw someone to smoke with, and for once congratulated himself on being at home; while Winnie — who was never comfortable in gloves and her newest frock, nor, it is to be inferred, directly affected by the restricted occupations of the Sabbath — her Saturday-night depression was considerably lessened by the news that the jolly uncle was going to stay until Monday morning. Poor Constance, in fact, was the one abstainer from the general welcome; but upon her, as usual, all the bother devolved; and when you picture her in the hot kitchen among the stupid women, doing what she could in the time, it should be permissible to sympathise with her, and to excuse her irritation, which was not decreased by the sight of all the others accompanying Uncle James round the garden, and by the sounds of the laughter coming through the kitchen window.

And indeed, the busy man's escape from the present pressing business, the sight of the old home he had not seen for twenty years, and the touch once more of his own dear girl's hand on his arm — though he had come to say goodbye to her — raised his spirits high enough to infect a parish. In this one it was a smaller performance to set the massed parishioners cock-a-hoop than to make their pastor chuckle and rub his hands. James Pontifex achieved the higher distinction.

"Ah, but I'm glad it's been raining," James exclaimed, sniffing satisfaction as they strolled in single file down a path which was under much water at the edges — James with his hand on his girl's shoulders. "The sight is good, but you get that sometimes; I've never forgotten the look of the old place; but what you never get is the smell. And how well you remember when you come back. Ah! I've sniffed no scent like this, Anthony, since when we were lads here together!"

"I wish we *had* been together," observed the Rector, with an emphasis which alluded good-humouredly to the thirteen years between them; "you show no signs of turning white, James."

"That's because I'm red," answered James gaily; "red don't bleach like black; you, I recollect, used to be as black as my boot."

The clergyman recollected too, and forgave the simile in the vision it evoked of himself in his young days. He had been a good-looking, though not a good-tempered young man. James had vivid memories of a thrashing he had received in those days for tampering with the big boy's razors when his razors were sacred novelties; he was about to mention it, but chose achievements of Anthony's less conspicuously devoid of lustre. The Rector took good humouredly such reminiscences; and few features of the garden failed to recall something to Anthony. Many were his joyful ejaculations over this and that landmark. The old trees were mostly the same, though grown; some old ones were gone, some new ones following up. The Roman coffins had been dug up since his day. Otherwise there was nothing new; not a new tile in the house, not a new flowerbed in the garden.

"And there's the old church, not a day older! But what's twenty years to it? Not half a day! I must have a look at it tomorrow."

"You were christened there," observed the Rector; and Camilla saw the font in the moonlight.

"They say in the village that you went up the tower by the lightning conductor," added Tony.

"Who says so?"

"Old Burrows."

"Old Burrows! There was a Burrows, certainly, but he was old as time in my day; is it the same, Anthony?"

"The very same; he was seventy then and is now ninety."

"I must see him tomorrow, too."

So they sauntered and chattered in the moist cool air until they could see no longer; and when they went in a dozen common objects of the garden, hitherto mere accessories in the scene, not particularly noticed, were looked on by Camilla as so many dumb friends from thenceforward. He had broken sentence after sentence to pour into her ears a gabble of Portuguese. She had greeted him in that language without correction; it seemed but natural of them to continue it; and the Rector, when James apologised, denied that there was any occasion for apology.

"I never saw the old boy in better form," Tony whispered. "Not that he could possibly *object* to their talking their own language together; but he was nice about it; the uncle's inspired him — and what a brick the uncle is!"

Winnie heartily assented; but Constance, after supper, expressed a characteristic opinion of certain exchanges of Portuguese at the table.

"It is not pleasant," said she, "to feel that you are being discussed before your face, in a language you do not understand. I don't say they were doing that, but they may have been, for all we know. In any case I call it bad manners."

Winnie called it nothing of the sort, and said so with more self-assertion than she often exhibited. "As if they would waste their time in talking about *us* — when they have only tomorrow together!"

"How do you know Camilla will stop?" Constance asked.

"Well, Uncle James very much wishes it; and we want to have her, I am sure; while as for Camilla — well, I *think* Camilla intends to stop."

"You think! You mean that you know; but I suppose her intentions [are] one of your precious secrets," replied Constance, with a jealous sneer. "I suppose it is you she can't tear herself away from. You're a lovely sight together, certainly — almost as touching as Camilla and her father."

Yet Constance had her softer side, though to most people it was the far side, and Winnie saw less of it than others. She sneered, certainly; but, though doubtless the discipline was good for her, and well-merited into the bargain, she had been left in the cold a good deal since the importation of Camilla; so at least there was human nature in her sneer. Nor did her scorn come from the heart; not, at any rate, as regarding

Camilla and her father. And her jealousy of Winnie was extended to Camilla and her father — less bitterly. [Yet] it *did* touch her to see them together — even on Sunday.

Constance played the organ in church — the other old church, at the far end of the village. It was not much of an organ, and it stood high up in the chancel, on the north side. On the same side, also in the chancel, was the vestry pew. When not playing Constance would turn her head towards the body of the church. She could see the pulpit without trouble — it was on that side too — and the reading desk without shifting her seat. But this morning her eye was arrested in its sweep before it came to the pulpit: it was arrested at the Rectory pew by the sight of Camilla and her father sitting there side by side. She watched them through both lessons and during most of the sermon: no one else could watch them at all. She saw the big man glancing downward at his daughter: she saw the pain in his face: she saw what no one else could see, the arm slipped round the girl's waist during the sermon. She had sneered at the "touching sight"; and its pathos was obvious, certainly; nevertheless it touched Constance on the Sunday morning, in spite of herself. Thereafter it moved her to a private sigh — free from bitterness — for which she felt no secret shame. As she watched, the harsh tones of her father, preaching perdition from his pulpit, fell all the time upon her ears. The contrast between the brothers — merely as parents — smote her heavily, and left a bruise.

She made an opportunity of speaking to Camilla after church. "Is he really going in the morning?" was all she said; but her tone was sympathetic.

"I am afraid so," answered Camilla; and there followed a sigh.

"And are you really...?"

"Yes. It is decided. Your father and mine talked it all over last night. It is decided."

"We wish to make you happy, dear," said Constance, kissing her forehead; "and, after all, a year soon passes."

"Does it? I am afraid I shall be a great trouble to you all. You are very good, Constance."

Constance, who suffered from gleams of self-revelation, which showed her the measure of her own goodness with cruel distinctness, turned away to hide her tears. But she left Camilla with unmoistened eyes; and Camilla had shrugged her shoulders repeatedly; and the impression was received, to be confirmed in the coolness of her normal moods, that Camilla was indifferent.

That young lady's fate was, as she herself said, decided; but had been virtually decided from the first. From the first she had been reconciled to the prospect of an unfamiliar life in surroundings which she could not conceive, among foreign relations whom she had never seen: blessed with an adaptable nature, she was prepared to make the best of the unknown, since her father so strongly wished it. In this spirit, and prepared for anything, she had in many things been delightfully disappointed. In her first letters to her father from Essingham she seemed contented to try these; in her later ones she seemed almost eager to do so; and as the Rector, at the hotel in London, but after a due deliberation, had rather more than consented to have her, the matter had really never been in doubt.

A talk between the brothers on the Saturday night had finally settled it. The man of business would be absent in Mozambique at least a year; he was privately certain it would be a long year; Camilla was to be a member of his brother's family until his return. Now that this was definitely settled, he confided in that brother his private provisions against the possibilities. He had settled on Camilla ten thousand pounds; besides leaving her everything, including his interest in the new Company by a will written in London. He gave his brother the names of the solicitors.

"And you are her legal guardian, Anthony, if I go to the crocodiles — her natural one meanwhile!"

"I have already promised," answered Anthony; for this was the important matter over which they had exchanged letters.

Guardianship, however, was not to be confounded with arbitrary control. The girl was to have what her uncle by no means approved of, a small escheat in care, and a banking account had already been opened for her at Hillston; she was to accompany her father to the bank there before his train left on Monday morning. Moreover, she must spend her money — this little income — as she liked. And if she wanted to travel to Lisbon in a year's time, she must go. "But I don't think she will want," said her father — "until I come back."

The Rector did not hesitate to say what he thought — that the child was being made a free spirit. James restricted the freedom, but trusted his child; she had an old head on her shoulders, he said; and in just one or two ways that was true. The Rector said no more about it; but he said a great deal about another well-meant but unfortunate idea of James's — which remained an idea. This was his suggestion to pay handsomely for Camilla's keep. The Rector flared up: the match had been applied to his family pride.

"If you think I can't afford to have her, leave her somewhere else, James — leave her somewhere else," he blurted out. "Haven't I told you she shall be as my own girls in your absence? Do you think, sir, that I want to make money of

112

her — out of my own niece?"

James seized his hand by way of answer, and wrung it.

"God bless you, Anthony! You are a good man — a good man. She is safe in your house — happy too, I never saw her happier. The little difference of religion is the only thing, but you are good about it — you are good — and there you know best. I never leant to the Catholics myself, though my dear wife.... But she is quite happy, and I, I leave her with a happy heart."

Nevertheless that Sunday, with its hot sun, its fresh breeze, and its sound of the old church bells, was one of the saddest in James Pontifex's life. The afternoon was saved from abject misery by Tony, who, after his sisters had gone to church, dragged Uncle James upstairs to his lair, to smoke. Camilla went with them, entering the room for the first time since the day when Tony got out the wine for her. And as she sat again on the arm of the big chair, with her father in it, and her hand upon his shoulder, that incident took softer outlines in her memory; Tony strode about the room, up and down his cage, after a habit of his, entertaining them to the top of his ability, which was not small, when he exerted [himself]; and once more she felt him as at first, her very kind friend; and reproached herself for having been unnecessarily indifferent with him for an inadequate cause. Felix was there too; James Pontifex petted him; and that imperfect little dog became dear to Camilla from that hour.

Tony and his uncle had taken to one another instantly. A fellow-feeling made them mutually kind. The bond developed conspiratorially over cigarettes after supper, when the uncle laid a hand on his nephew's shoulder, and said suddenly:

"My boy, I fear you take too closely after *me*."

"I'm glad to hear it," murmured Tony, laughing.

113

"You needn't be glad; I was a wild young idiot at your age; from what your father has told me, you are just a little bit wild too — or have been. Well, if you will let me advise you, you will give one thing among others a wide berth — the race course. I didn't."

"I know what my father has been telling you," exclaimed the young man; "but I haven't backed a horse for more than a year. I had an immense stroke of luck about a year ago, and I haven't been near a racecourse since. It is very unsportsmanlike — getting up from the table the moment you win — but I promised the governor, and I have kept my promise."

"There are other snares," Mr James suggested.

Tony was silent. His uncle took him by the arm.

"My dear fellow, I don't want to lecture you. But I know what it is — I know the signs also — your father is his father to say all this over again; and it had the same effect on me. I don't know why I didn't go entirely to the bad. Yet I do know. My marriage saved me. But you mustn't wait for that, my boy. Are you offended?"

Tony answered, with honest emotion, that he was not.

"Don't you wait on that, my boy... I was one in a thousand for luck and mercy — I married one in ten million. I have only seen one other like her: the daughter I am leaving behind me tomorrow! Through mercy which I did not deserve, and cannot understand, I sowed wild oats, yet never reaped the whirlwind. But it is right that we reap as we sow — and the rule — my case was the exception. Do remember this: study now, my dear boy: if you do not feel fitted for the Church — and I respect your honesty there — do settle down striving for something when you leave Cambridge. If you must leave the country, come out to me. Whatever you do, I am your friend.

Will you forgive me for saying so — and many other things?"

The young fellow was intensely moved. He grasped the other's hand.

"Forgive you? You don't know what a brute you make me feel, but I thank you — I thank you from my heart. I am worse, I dare say, than you ever were. But I *will* settle down. You don't know how you have helped me. If only my father was more like you I mightn't need your help so much! I'm a brute, but I'll try to do better, I will indeed. And I'll see to Camilla; she'll have a good time if I can help to give her one: she's my new sister."

"There are many ways in which you can help."

"Tell me one!"

"Well, she has not the religion in her that her mother had — that's a fact, God forgive me. But she would sometimes like to go to her own church. Your father has promised to throw no positive obstacle in the way; but naturally enough he will not assist her to go; and I only thought that some day, without causing any trouble, *you* might see your way — "

"Of course I might!"

"Just to satisfy her!"

"Trust me to arrange it."

"You're a good fellow, Tony."

"I tell you I'm her new brother."

"God bless you! That comes glibly enough; I wish there were more behind it. You told my girl you weren't religious, and it distressed her; how would it distress her if she knew I were not either!"

And yet —

Camilla woke that night to find her father in her room, praying at the side of the bed. She flung her arms round his neck, and drew him to her. The light of the waning moon

115

came dimly through the blind, and lay like [a drab pall] on the bed, and for months afterwards, when the moon fell so, Camilla would wake and see him then, and hear his dear voice, choked with tears.

# Chapter XII: *Untitled*

Camilla's least attractive trait, her apparent callousness, became, after her father's final departure, still more plain to superficial students of her character. Her uncle, cold as he was, remarked her well-bred mien and manner with a surprise which was not wholly pleasant; like many cold men, he could appreciate what he repelled — an exhibition of affection; and he would have liked Camilla none the worse had her eyes been red and her feet heavy for a day or two. But all such symptoms of a natural sorrow were conspicuous only by their absence; and Mr Pontifex, who had given her a great many games of bagatelle on the Monday afternoon, decided that the consolation was unnecessary; though, as she seemed fond of the game, this did not prevent him from playing with her again in the evening. The rattle of the balls penetrated the schoolroom, with an occasional sound which would not have been heard had Mr Pontifex been playing with one of his daughters — a sound of laughter. Those young ladies, as a rule, and one with very few exceptions, had neither the inclination, nor even the temerity, to laugh aloud in their father's company. If Camilla could do so now — with her own father newly gone, whose contrast with theirs was privately felt by both girls — well, they could not understand. Winnie did not profess to do so; she only professed affection; but her sister had prepared herself for an inconsolable Camilla, and the sympathy with which, for once, she had been ready, oozed away. She had already labelled Camilla indifferent; now she attached a stronger string to that label.

[ *At this point the narrative comes to a halt.* ]

# Manuscript

General observations

As noted at the outset, the first chapter's opening page is a mess. That chapter is written in pencil, as are the second and third, but the three that follow are in ink. The seventh and eighth are in pencil but the ninth and tenth are in ink. The eleventh and the opening paragraph of the twelfth are once again in pencil. These drafts suggest that Hornung's working practice (on this occasion, at any rate) was to scribble out a chapter in pencil, while the white heat of creation was upon him, and then — after reviewing and revising it at leisure — to write it out again in ink. The original text was for his eyes alone while the second, more presentable "fair copy" version, was intended, ultimately, for the printer.

The pencil texts overflow with revisions whereas they come, not surprisingly, far less frequently in the inked texts. One crucial difference to be noted at the outset is that Anthony Pontifex is referred to as "the rector" in the pencil text but as "the Rector" in the inked version. (The only exception to this rule, easily explained, occurs in the seventh chapter.) The important point to note about the author's eventual adoption of the capital letter is that the small "r" was still being used in the opening paragraph of the twelfth chapter: Hornung was clearly uncertain, for the moment, how to proceed with his story after writing that paragraph, but he did *not* then put the book to one side. While mulling the matter over, he went back to the earlier sections of the text and wrote out again, in ink, five of the previous chapters. (Those that he did *not* re-write at this stage were evidently in need of more radical revision, to bring them into line with subsequent developments, and he needed time to reflect on how best this could be done.)

The author numbered each page in its top right-hand corner.

He also intended — from the third chapter on, at any rate — to supply every chapter with a title, but only got so far as devising five that (provisionally) seemed appropriate. These are noted below, as we consider the manuscript on a chapter-by-chapter basis to get a fuller notion of how the story was being shaped and the occasional problems encountered — and Hornung's consequent changes and instructions to himself. We are, as it were, looking over his shoulder for the whole time. (For ease of reference, a synopsis of each chapter has been supplied.) Just to complicate things for the reader, it must be confessed that a good many sentences deleted by Hornung have been reinstated by the present editor — but the places where this has been done are indicated.

Chapter I, seemingly untitled (MS pages 1 to 20; in pencil)

*Synopsis*: James Pontifex, a widower of fifty, and Camilla, his seventeen-year-old daughter, are waiting in their room at a Trafalgar Square hotel for the arrival of his brother, the Rector of Essingham. It is an early evening in late August. James has lived in Lisbon for many years and has returned to England after a long absence. To his daughter, motherless since the age of six, it is a totally strange country but she has a fairly good English vocabulary. The Rector, Anthony Pontifex, arrives. He is older than James and is actually his half-brother. He is also a widower and has two grown-up daughters. It soon becomes apparent that, in contrast to James's cheerfulness, he is an austere, strait-laced character with virtually no sense of humour. He is also a teetotaler. Camilla, rather abashed by her uncle's icy demeanour, is sent down to the reading room while they talk in private. James explains that he has a great favour to ask. He has become involved in the establishment of a new sugar-planting company in Mozambique and, in addition to raising capital in Britain for this venture, proposes to go out to that country for at least a year. Since the African climate would be too hot for his daughter, he hopes

119

that Anthony will agree to look after her during that period. Anthony establishes that the girl has been brought up as a Catholic, which rather shocks him, but decides, that night, that he will accept the challenge and do all he can to convert her to the Protestant faith.

On page 1, Camilla was first of all described as "a girl of seventeen", just as she had been in the opening sentence of the aborted scrap of text. On reflection, Hornung changed "seventeen" to "eighteen". But elsewhere (i.e., on pages 96, 97 and 161, where she is "some five years younger" than her cousin Tony) she would revert to being a seventeen-year-old, so that is the age that has been editorially adopted.

On the next page, he deleted the final three sentences of the opening paragraph (i.e., everything that follows the word "Square") but they have been editorially restored — and the words "thirty-five minutes past six o'clock" have also been editorially inserted (where a space had been left previously), since we learn, later, that the theatres are due to open within an hour or so. On the same page, Camilla exclaims "*Está minto tarde*" ["He is late"]. It may be recalled that this was what appeared in large writing on the first page: Hornung's knowledge of the Portuguese language was very limited, and he required assistance when he wanted to use it: somebody in the family circle had supplied him with those words. (It is just conceivable, of course, that those words were intended to serve as a title.)

Individual words, or sometimes whole sentences, are deleted or substantially amended in the pages that follow. In the paragraph dealing with James's early life (page 3), there had originally appeared the sentence "The lines of James Pontifex had fallen twenty years ago in foreign waters, and he had never changed his fishing ground, this one had yielded" — to be struck through instantly and replaced by a longer sentence conveying what are essentially the same sentiments, while over the deleted sentence were inserted the words "His wishes fathered the opposite thought."

A paragraph break (page 4) has been editorially introduced with the words "Now Camilla, who resembled her father so little", mainly to reduce the jarring impact of one "now" following close upon the heels of another. (The second "Now" had been inserted as an afterthought.) After a subsequent sentence ending with the words "was itself something special." there originally appeared the following passage:

> [*Four indecipherable words*] from Lisbon; but at last dragged his anchor out of the Tagus in a year's absence at least from Europe which had become necessary: he was about to leave his daughter in England if this could be arranged; this was enough to sadden even a cheerful widower, when he had spare moments in which to think about it. Luckily he had not many; but the present moments were an instalment, and an unexpected one, which ultimately ended

The deletion tails off when it reaches the words "in an abrupt uprising". (A "Yet" has been editorially inserted as a means of breaching the gap.) Hornung had decided, obviously, that too much of the plot was being revealed too soon, and that it would be better to leave the reader in suspense for a little longer. It would, in any case, be more sensible to unveil the facts of the situation when James starts talking to his brother, rather than narrate them twice over.

On pages 5 and 6, a line is casually struck through the text (between "believed himself to be." and "Camilla replied confidently"), but the purpose of this line is not clear and the text has been allowed to stand. On page 8, the reference to Camilla colouring in patches, "like rose-leaves", has also been struck through, but this too has been allowed to stand. The sentence "Indeed, the expression with which he regarded her delicate beauty was almost as stony as that provoked by the room." was a late insertion.

On page 9, the initial exchanges between the two brothers have been deleted, so that their talk starts abruptly with the question "But why send her out at all?" which obviously does not make sense. The deleted exchanges have therefore been restored.

At the bottom of page 11, when James has cautiously broached the subject of his daughter, there comes the sentence "Now I am here, then, what about her?" This had originally read "'Well, since I *am* here,' said Anthony, dryly, 'what about her?'" And at this point the author hesitated. There was still an inch to spare at the bottom of the page, but Hornung needed to break off from his narrative for a time. He therefore jotted down the words "her history — ends by saying he must go. Don't want to have her there: Anthony will you take care of her for me[?]" — and inserted "have 2 girls of your own" over the top of the final six words. (A further compressed reminder to himself of some other point, in very small writing, was hived off in the bottom left-hand corner of the page, but the opening words "It is" are all that the present writer has managed to decipher.)

The remaining nine pages of this chapter (12 to 21) contain minor adjustments and deletions but nothing of any great significance — beyond the fact that the narrator indicates (page 15), in a late addition, that Anthony is about thirty years behind the times in his puritanical viewpoint.

It will be helpful, before going further, to try to establish the basic chronology in slightly more detail — as Hornung himself would have done before starting his book. James, we are told elsewhere, is thirteen years younger than his brother, which means that his brother is aged sixty-three. Assuming (for reasons to be explained later) that the action in this chapter is taking place in 1894, then it follows that Anthony was born in

1831. Anthony's mother having died (in 1842 or thereabouts), his father had married again and a second son, James, had arrived on the scene in 1844. James left home thirty years later. It must be assumed that, possibly after brief visits to other parts of the world, he had arrived in Lisbon in 1875, where he met and fell in love with a beautiful girl, the daughter of an impoverished Portuguese Count. They marry and Camilla, their daughter, is born in 1877. They also have a son, who is either stillborn or dies very young. We know that James's wife had died in 1882, since he had been a widower for twelve years, and it may be that this was as a result of giving birth to their son.

## Chapter II, untitled (MS pages 21 to 39; in pencil)

*Synopsis:* Next morning, the Rector sends a telegram to his home. It reaches Essingham ninety minutes later and is received in the garden by Winnie Pontifex, his younger daughter. She dutifully takes it to her sister Constance, who exercises general control over the household arrangements. Constance expresses displeasure at the news that the Rector will be bringing their unknown cousin home with him that evening. We learn that Winnie is plump and plain but sensible and sensitive, whereas Constance is strikingly beautiful but short-tempered, rather impatient and somewhat domineering. A visit that afternoon from a young High Church rector based in a neighbouring parish (a Mr Atkinson) puts her in a good mood The two travellers eventually arrive and there is an austere family meal. Camilla, exhausted after the long journey, retires to her room. At evening prayers (a rather grim event) the Rector is displeased to note that two of the male servants are missing. He is also annoyed by the fact that his son, another Anthony, is absent and that his sisters have no idea of his whereabouts. When the servants have left the dining-room, he reveals to the girls, in stern and awesome solemnity, the dreadful news that Camilla is a Roman Catholic. He declares that he

123

will do all he can to save her from perdition and win her over to the Protestant faith. Later, peeping in at Camilla's door, the girls find that she has fallen asleep by her bedside, praying on her knees. Constance is contemptuous and Winnie is compassionate. At this point there is the sound of an angry voice from the downstairs hall.

The chapter has got off to an exhilarating start, as we follow the progress of the telegram from London to Hillston, the market-town of an unspecified county, and the adventures of the dilatory telegraph boy on his four-mile journey from there to the village of Essingham. After being confined to the slightly stuffy atmosphere of a hotel in the opening chapter, the reader is lyrically transported into the fresh air and attractions of a countryside abundant in pine trees and rabbits. The scenery and the action has "broadened out", as it were, into pastures new, and there is an element of panache in the narrative.

Before looking in detail at the manuscript, however, it might be as well to recall the opening words of the first of the two notes which have come down to us, namely:

> Here at all events she will live strictly & quietly. English home life. Opportunities to think & to reflect, or to profit by example; and no friction, I hope no frivolities to distract. It is a responsibility for us all. Lead her in the right way.

These words are not identical to those which the Rector used in addressing his daughters towards the end of the chapter, but in essence they convey the same message. What is of rather more interest, however, is the fact that Hornung had headed that note with the words "Chapter I". This obviously suggests that he had originally intended to begin his novel with what has now become the *second* chapter. But rather than having to listen to the Rector supply to his daughters, at one stage removed, an account of what had taken place at that hotel interview, the reader has now been allowed to hear it first-hand.

The pages that follow contain some minor corrections and refinements but nothing of any great significance. The text flows freely, with only a few subsequent alterations. A small billiard-table in the hall is changed (eventually) to a bagatelle-board (pages 27 and 30). The unflattering description (page 28) of poor Winnie is slightly enhanced, for whereas we are told, initially, that "her muscles were those of a man", an amplified version reads "her wrists and muscles were as those of a man". When the Rector breaks the news to his daughters about Camilla's religion (page 35), his speech originally began with the announcement that he had "a nasty thing to inform you of respecting your cousin..." but this is revised to read "an unpleasant thing to tell you respecting your cousin ...". Their reactions to his news (page 36) were at first described in just one sentence:

> The information duly affected both girls: Winnie opened her soft eyes wide, and Constance could not restrain a little gasp of horror.

On reflection, Hornung changed "and" to "but". He also added what appears to be another sentence but, maddeningly, the writing is so small that it is impossible to decipher his jottings with guaranteed accuracy. It appears to begin with the words "They gazed at [their] father", followed by "had heard such things", and ends with "furrows fill crow; the black shadows." This is gibberish as it stands, and must have been serving as a kind of shorthand to jog the author's memory when he came to write out his fair-copy version of the text. (A rather lame editorial substitute simply says "They gazed at their father as if stunned by such black news.") Later (page 37), the Rector speaks of rescuing Camilla from "heresy", but this is changed to "false doctrine".

Adjustments to the remaining text are minimal. It should be noted, perhaps, that the page numbering has been changed after page 33: page 34 had previously been 36, and so on to the end of the chapter. It may be that a couple of pages were cancelled or it may simply have been a numbering error on the part of the author, instantly corrected.

In passing, one might be permitted to raise a puzzled eyebrow at the fact that the Rectory is the Pontifex family home at Essingham, where both Anthony and James had been born. It is an unusual arrangement, perhaps, as the post of Rector is not hereditary, but it must be assumed that Mr Pontifex senior had also been the Rector of the parish and that such a "succession" had seemed convenient to the ecclesiastical authorities — and Hornung does describe Essingham, indeed, as "the family living", though the term is being used in a more literal sense than usual.


Chapter III, 'A Clergyman's Son' (MS pages 40 to 52; in pencil)

*Synopsis:* The Rector is enraged to discover that his son Anthony (referred to henceforth as 'Tony') has been playing cards in the stables with the two male servants missing at evening prayers. He frog-marches him into the house, expostulating loudly. Tony ruefully explains to his two sisters, as he is paraded past, that they had simply been playing for pennies. Constance feels it serves Tony right whereas Winnie is more sympathetic towards her brother. There follows a description of Tony, confined to his room with the company of Felix, his fox-terrier. He is now twenty-two and has been subjected to the domineering behaviour of his father since the death of his mother, fourteen years earlier. He is basically a good-natured young man but is developing some rebellious traits, both at Cambridge University and at home, and inclined to be lazy. Winnie calls in to comfort him, but brings with her the news that the two servants have been dismissed. Tony is less affectionate towards his sister than he might be, treating her in a careless fashion, and has no great interest in the news of Camilla's arrival. As Winnie goes out of the door, he is privately feasting his eyes on the picture of a young actress (scantily-clad, presumably) dressed as Cleopatra.

It was apparently at the commencement of this chapter that Hornung decided that each of his chapters would require a title. No space had been allowed for chapter-headings so far as Chapters I and II were concerned, but with Chapter III the title "A Clergyman's Son" came (one assumes) instantly to mind. Sufficient space for titles would be left, henceforth, underneath each of the numbered chapters.

The relevant facts that Hornung had jotted down on the second of his two notes have all been incorporated in this chapter, namely:

> Is spending the long at Cambridge, reading: home for day or two. Will go back *before* breakfast.

> Further reference to hussy-gazing.

> He had played the rather commonplace part of wild undergrad.

— although there has been, in the event, no previous reference to "hussy-gazing".

There are some minor changes and corrections in the scribbled text but none of any great consequence: most of the words deleted reappear a line or two later.

Reverting to the subject of chronology, based on our surmise that the action is taking place in 1894, we now know that Tony had been born in 1872 and Winnie in 1874 and that their mother had died in 1880. It is not clear when Constance was born: we are told that she is older than Winnie but not whether she is also older than Tony. It would require a leap of the imagination to envisage the Rector marrying for love, and one which we are not required to make: it is explained that he had done so primarily for business reasons, in order to enhance the acreage of the family living, and had made the sacrifice of marrying slightly beneath him — hence the coarseness in Winnie's appearance.


## Chapter IV, untitled (MS pages 53 to 74; in ink)

*Synopsis*: It is the following morning and breakfast-time in the Pontifex household. Camilla scandalises the Rector by saying that she prefers wine to either tea or coffee: he declares that wine is banned from the Rectory. Glumly, Camilla goes to her room and starts writing a letter to her father. The two sisters adjourn to the school-room and bicker slightly: Constance takes the Rector's part, while Winnie thinks he is far too stern towards both Tony and their guest. A young man called Erskine Hope looks in at the window to pass the time of day. Camilla joins them and mistakes the young man for Tony, whom she has not yet met. (The actual Tony had set off for Cambridge before breakfast.) Erskine, a student at Oxford, is the son of wealthy Lady Harriett, a nearby neighbour (a widow for twenty years). He is en route to meet the local doctor to discuss cricket arrangements, but is clearly much attracted by Camilla. Winnie accompanies him for part of the way. Constance, in a kindly mood, meanwhile tells Camilla about the Hopes and advises her on English phraseology, explaining that it is inappropriate to describe Erskine as "pretty". Their sunnier mood of friendship is spoilt, however, when Constance notes, with disapproval, that Camilla is wearing some amber beads, hitherto semi-concealed. Camilla explains that they were a gift from her mother and that her peace of mind would be disturbed if she removed them. Constance wrongly equates this belief with idolatrous practices but Camilla simply shrugs her shoulders, convinced that she will be unable to make her cousin understand her point of view. Their exchanges are curtailed when the gong rings for lunch.

As indicated above, this text is a "fair copy", replacing the original pencilled version. There are a few minor alterations in the first seven pages (53 to 59), with the odd word changed or deleted, but nothing worth recording. On pages 60 and 61, however, one finds that a line has been drawn through most of the dialogue between the two sisters (starting with the words "Then perhaps you know" and ending with "Whatever they are"). This implies that the abridged text would have run:

"So I *know*!"
"He has never been anything but kind and generous to us both," etc.

but, wisely or otherwise, the deletion has been ignored by the present editor.

Similarly, another line has been drawn through most of the dialogue on page 62 and the opening lines on page 63 (starting with the words "If he is betting and gambling" and ending with "drinking with the men."). This implies that the abridged text would have run:

"My impression is," said Constance, who had borne her rebuke with ostentatious patience, "that none of us know the worst of him!"
But Winnie let her have the last word, which, indeed, was the only thing to do with Constance; etc.

But, once again, the deleted dialogue has been allowed to stand by the present editor. The remaining eleven pages (64 to 74) contain only very minor changes and deletions, none of them worth recording.

## Chapter V, untitled (MS pages 75 to 93; in ink)

*Synopsis:* Erskine Hope and his mother are extremely fond of each other and both delight in the company of young women. Erskine has some feminine characteristics, both in personality and appearance (partially justifying Camilla's use of the word "pretty"). But he plays cricket, which establishes his manly credentials. Winnie, accompanying him down the drive, is clearly smitten. For his part, Erskine is smitten by Camilla, but manages to conceal this from Winnie, whom he regards as "a good sort" but not much more. She tells him all she knows of the new arrival. He calls at the Dispensary to finalise cricket arrangements for the following day with the local doctor. Returning to the Hall, he is good-humouredly interrogated about Camilla by his mother, who speedily realises that he is developing yet another infatuation. Mischievously inclined, Lady Harriett says she will manoeuvre the Rector into inviting them to dinner so that she can assess the young woman, and the way she is being treated, for herself. She puts this plan into effect the following day, much to the Rector's irritation, since he does not greatly care for Lady Harriett's company. Camilla is intrigued by her brief glimpse of the visitor and, in conversation with Constance, admires her striking white hair. Constance tells her that Lady Harriett had been dyeing her hair until a year ago, when a young man living nearby had persuaded her to desist. Constance is laughingly contemptuous of him but says that she will invite him to the dinner-party as well. She adds that the young man in question (who will prove to be a Mr Atkinson) is somebody whom the Rector likes, despite being High Church. The reader learns that he is paying court to Constance herself.

Here again, this text is a "fair copy", replacing the original pencilled version, but further revisions were still being made. Sometimes Hornung adjusted the text as he wrote while a handful of later corrections, in very small writing, are lightly inserted with a sharp pencil. There is a minor change to the chapter's second sentence (page 75), when "at all events in silhouette" is changed to "at least in outline". Describing Erskine's restrained reactions to Winnie's praise of Camilla (page 80), the words "it was not his nature to do so" are replaced by "that sort of thing did not come easily to him". Some words jotted down at the top of this page, perhaps as a possible alternative, appear to read "he enthused, as the S joked, 'too dutifully'". Clearly, the author was trying to capture a precise shade of meaning. (Could the "S" have stood for Sage?)

When they part company, preoccupied by very different thoughts and desires, attention is drawn, once again (and rather unkindly), to Winnie's large hands. The subject of "hands" seems to have held a particular interest for Hornung. On page 86, Erskine takes his mother's plump hand within his arm, the adjective "plump" being a subsequent addition.

When Erskine leaves the Dispensary and approaches the Hall (page 83), he passes one other person to whom he has "plenty to say". This is a rather curious incident, since we are not told *what* he said and the description of that person ("a dirty old gentleman in a smock-frock and one of Erskine's own silk hats") was inserted as an afterthought. He may simply have been chatting to one of the deserving poor, so that his affability and good-nature are seen to full advantage, or it could be that this mysterious character was intended to reappear at a later stage.

Discussing Winnie's possible emotional attraction to her son, the sentence "He doesn't see this" (page 88) was a late arrival in Lady Harriett's thoughts. Intent on securing for them both a dinner invitation to the Rectory as soon as possible, she announces (page 89) that she will call at the Rectory "this very afternoon" — which was later amended to read "tomorrow, while you are playing cricket". A second consequent revision came on page 90, when Lady Harriett originally visited the Rectory "after the nap" — three words which had to be deleted.

The cricket match would have been on a Saturday. This alerts us to the fact that *all* the events covered in this chapter were originally planned to take place on the Friday. But Hornung would have been aware that he was still only into the third day of his narrative and that it was desirable to speed up the passage of time. (Camilla's father has several business calls to make before he re-enters the story, and he needs adequate room in which to do so.) So the final section of this chapter (from the point where Lady Harriett "duly" makes her call) takes place on the Saturday afternoon. (Having established, retrospectively, that the late-August meeting in that Trafalgar Square hotel had taken place on a Wednesday evening, and bearing in mind the notion that 1894 was the year in question, it would not be unreasonable to assume that the story had commenced on 29 August and that the date we had now reached was the first of September. But in the next chapter, after being informed that a week had elapsed since Camilla's arrival, we are told that it is still August — which obliges us to backdate the starting-point of the narrative to Wednesday, 22 August.)

The dinner-party is arranged "for an evening of the following week" which, in the event, will prove to be (by the calculations outlined above) Thursday, the 30th.

Camilla, the author wrote initially (page 91), "had felt the old lady's eyes upon her much of the time, without their" but then halted. He changed "felt" to "met" and inserted the word "interested" in front of "eyes, emphatically deleted the eight words which followed "eyes", and continued his sentence with the words "more than once, and felt them all the time." Later, in very light pencil and tiny writing, he added a cryptic remark which appears to read "Her name [or 'mane'?] was difficult to [put the strong pen to?] had of silent h's —" which is a reflection that, so far as the present editor is concerned, must remain totally impenetrable.

Discussing Lady Harriett's hair (page 92), Constance's remark "Dyes it, my dear!" was a late insertion. A peripheral character would shortly be re-entering the story, and the treatment of her ladyship's hair provides a rather unexpected opportunity to prepare the way for his second appearance. "And only fancy," Constance exclaims, "it was quite a young man — a High Church clergyman living near here — who persuaded her to desist from dyeing it. At her age —" At which point the author paused and revised his sentence. All the words after "quite a young man" were scored through with much emphasis. He replaced them by "living near here, who persuaded her to give up dyeing her hair — and she old enough to be his mother!" The revelation that the young man is High Church is held back until the last moment, and Constance does not mention his actual profession to Camilla. Hornung promptly identifies him (page 93) as the "young clergyman" already glimpsed fleetingly in the second chapter — but the word "clergyman" is instantly deleted and replaced by "ritualistic rector".

There was a need to differentiate between two rectors based in the same locality, which accounts for the author's decision to refer to Anthony Pontifex as "the Rector" (with a capital 'R') and his eldest daughter's suitor as "the rector" (with a small one).


## Chapter VI, untitled (MS pages 94 to 115; in ink)

*Synopsis:* James Pontifex and his brother exchange letters about how Camilla is settling down. James is assured, both by the Rector and by Camilla herself, that all is going well. A week has elapsed since her arrival and Camilla has spent some "quality" time with each member of the family, who (in their individual ways) have done their best to make her welcome. Under the guidance of the two sisters, she starts to explore the area. There are two churches — a functional one at the far end of the village and the much more ancient one of All Souls, now disused and falling into partial disrepair, alongside the Rectory. The latter attracts her and she returns there alone one afternoon. Her necklace of amber beads disintegrates as she is sitting in a pew, the threading cord having broken, which greatly distresses her. But she has barely, with much guilt, started to gather them up, being anxious to conceal them from other members of the family (and, above all, from the Rector), when a cheerful young man enters the church  and introduces himself as her cousin Tony. (Newly-returned to Essingham, we are told later.)  He shows her around and she is impressed by the apparent depth of his knowledge, but he confesses at length that this is simply information that he has acquired haphazardly from more erudite visitors. Talking about the family, he recalls that her father was renowned, in his day, as being quite a scamp. Camilla, in return, tells him about her life in Lisbon and the gambling activities of her reckless old grandfather. They both burst into laughter and at this point the Rector enters, in high dudgeon, and expels them from the building. Tony once again finds himself in disgrace with his father — who, later, makes it emphatically clear that he will be disowned should he marry an actress, a barmaid or a Roman Catholic.

Like its two predecessors, this text is a "fair copy", replacing the original pencilled version. Its twenty-two pages (94 - 115) contain only minor refinements and alterations, none of any great moment, and only three points are worth noting.

On the opening page (94) an inch of space was left within which a title could later be inserted. The possibility of calling this chapter "Essingham All Souls" occurred to the author and he pencilled in those words in the top right-hand corner, but perhaps with no great enthusiasm. It was something to bear in mind if nothing more striking materialised.

It suddenly occurred to Hornung, perhaps with an eye to future developments, that Tony's dog Felix should be playing a more active role in the action.  On the bottom (blank) half of the final page (115) there appear the following jottings:

[*In very large writing*]
Senhor Felix

Senhora Camilla

[*In much smaller writing*]
Felix
let me introduce you — I call him F because

"I am already his friend."

"Mine too?  Run together."

One can envisage a scene in which, as the couple leave the ancient church, the little fox-terrier comes rushing up to them and Tony effects the whimsical introductions, only to find that Camilla and Felix are already great pals.  Felix is in a playful mood, and as he scampers off Tony urges Camilla to chase after him.  But, as the text stands, the sudden irruption of the Rector rules out such an episode and it would be necessary to find an alternative location for it.  (In Chapter IX Tony will invite Camilla into his room and point to a vacant armchair as being the usual seat of "your friend Felix", momentarily forgetting that the reader has not been told of this friendship.  And in Chapter XI, to slightly complicate matters further, we will be told that Felix only became "dear" to Camilla from the moment that her father patted him — although this is not necessarily incompatible with the notion that they had simply been friends until that point.)

So far as the passage of time is concerned, we learn that "the first week" has gone by since Camilla's arrival.  That had been on a Thursday evening (surmised to be 23 August).  It is therefore assumed that the events covered in this chapter, preceding the Rectory dinner-party, are taking place on the second Thursday (i.e., 30 August).

## Chapter VII, 'Very Small Talk' (MS pages 116 to 132; in pencil)

*Synopsis:* Despite the absence of wine, the dinner-party with the Hopes goes off surprisingly well. Constance has arranged things very deftly. Erskine is charming and extremely attentive to Camilla. Tony is relatively quiet and so too is Winnie. Camilla is privately anxious to return to the church to collect her scattered beads. The Rector (in a good mood, after playing bagatelle with her) is an amicable host and his relations with Lady Harriett are unexpectedly congenial. He is startled to learn that Camilla, in her own country, had attended bull-fights "Sunday after Sunday", but keeps silent on the matter. He is even more startled, however, to find that she has been accustomed to play cards for money, but Lady Harriett smooths things over. Dismissing the notion of cards, she persuades Camilla to sing to them and the young lady proves to have a striking voice. Constance (hitherto regarded as the singer of the family) is rather jealous and annoyed that Mr Atkinson, the tall young rector and, seemingly, her acknowledged beaux, should be impressed by her cousin. The Rector is equally impressed by his niece's ability. Lady Harriett, taking her leave, surreptitiously invites Camilla to come and play cards with her at the Hall (bringing her purse) and Erskine squeezes her hand tightly.

This is again a pencilled first draft, unlike the three chapters which have preceded it, and rather more scrappy in appearance. In the space reserved for a chapter-heading (page 116), the words "Very Small Talk" have been lightly inserted, suggesting that the author was not altogether certain about this title. The chapter begins with the words "Tony saw no m—"

but these are instantly struck through. Wishing to preserve an air of detachment, and not to be seen favouring one character more than another, the author began again underneath with the words "Young Pontifex saw no more ..."

It would seem that Hornung was experiencing a change of heart towards the Rector. Having been grimness personified during the first six chapters, the reverend gentleman now demonstrates that he is capable of lighter moments and even of positive forbearance at times when he might be expected to explode with wrath. Bearing in mind that he had been berating the luckless Tony at the end of Chapter VI about the iniquity of Roman Catholics, it is rather extraordinary — or, at any rate, slightly erratic — to find that he had been playing bagatelle with Camilla immediately after this confrontation. On reflection, Hornung might well have decided to revise this section of the book so that the mellowing does not come so abruptly.

When the slightly over-attentive Erskine escorts Camilla into dinner, while her thoughts tend to be preoccupied by Tony, the words "excluded Winnie" appear in the top right-hand corner of the page (119). When it comes to Camilla's views on bull-fights (page 120), she exclaims in the first instance "I think them delightful." This did not seem quite right, and Hornung changed the adjective to "dreadful". But this too was instantly deleted, being replaced by "charming". In amplification of her subsequent remarks, it may be noted that *cavaleiros* (attired in 18th century costume) fight the bull from horseback, seeking to stab three or four small javelins (*bandarilhas*) in their backs, while *bandarilheiros*, on foot, are similar to Spanish *matadores* but torment the bulls with red cloaks. In neither case do the fighters seek to inflict mortal or lasting damage on their victims.

The absence of wine from the dinner-table (page 122) was a subject about which the author was almost incensed. "Tacitly to deny this or that to your adult guests," he declared, "on the ground just that it is wrong, is to offer them obvious insult." Clearly, he was smarting under just such an insult (or a recollection of one) as he wrote those words. But, on reflection, he decided not to labour the point, and his private views are in any case made adequately clear in more restrained terms.

There are a number of changes and deletions in the remaining pages of this chapter, but none of them of any great importance. Three pages are renumbered — what is now 126 had originally been 127, what is now 127 had originally been 128 and what is now 129 had originally been 130. Page 128 (coming between pages 127 and 129, as renumbered) had not borne any previous number, however, which suggests that this page had been inserted as a replacement. Another point worth mentioning, bearing in mind that this is a "pencilled" chapter, is that the word "Rector" appears with a capital 'R' on page 126 — the only instance in the manuscript where this happens — which reinforces the notion that some re-writing had taken place.

If Mr Atkinson had followed Constance's lofty advice, and looked up the word "sordine" in the dictionary, he would have found that it meant a mute for musical instruments: making clear, in other words, that in Constance's opinion Camilla had been singing far too loudly.


Chapter VIII, title not finalised (MS pages 133 to 148; in pencil)

*Synopsis:* Constance remains irritated because of the praise bestowed upon Camilla's singing. Reading in bed at midnight, she is surprised to receive a visit from the young lady herself, in an agitated state because she has not yet managed to retrieve her scattered beads from the old church. She relates her woes, but Constance is largely unsympathetic. Half an hour later, Camilla resolves to slip across to the church by herself. It proves a more hazardous and frightening visit than anticipated, and she is distressed at not being able to find her beads. Tony (having spotted her from his window) once again appears on the scene, to her immense joy and relief. He calms her down and escorts her back to the house, reflecting that this is a very rum instance of sleep-walking.

This too is a pencilled first draft, as scrappy in appearance as its predecessor. The space reserved for a chapter-heading (page 133) has been left blank for the moment, but four possibilities have been jotted down — "Wilful Folly" and "Camilla's Folly" in the upper-left corner, "The Resolution of a Capacity for Woolgathering" partially over "Chapter VIII" and "*Sub Nocte*" underneath that.

The narrative flows on smoothly, with only minor alterations as the author proceeded. The sentence reflecting on "the clownish suggestion of Mr Atkinson" was inserted as an afterthought, at the top of page 135. The "twinge" that Constance felt as Camilla took her leave (page 137) appears originally to have been one "of compassion" — for those two words have been very thoroughly squiggled through (as distinct from being merely deleted by two or three strokes), as though the author were ashamed of having written them, and can only be deciphered with difficulty. Camilla (also page 137) originally said "Good night, Constance. Thank you." — but the two final words were deleted.

As Camilla reflects (page 140) on "what Constance had said, with her manner of saying it," there at first followed the words "increased her desire until it burned in her bosom, with a consuming heat in which nerves and common sense" — but these were deleted, the sentence continuing with "concentrated that willfulness from which she was not free, etc."

The paragraph in which she frantically hunts in the (wrong) pew for her missing beads (page 145), and despairs at being unable to find them, attracted a note at the bottom of the page, in large letters, "one more sign of X", which does not convey a great deal to the present editor. On the subsequent page, as indicated in the text, the author left clear a couple of lines in which he could insert some Portuguese utterances of despair. (Once, of course, somebody had been found to supply them.)

The two final short paragraphs in this chapter (page 148), describing Tony's reactions, are in very small writing so that they might be squeezed into the limited space available. They were presumably inserted as afterthoughts, to pave the way for the opening paragraph of the next chapter.

Chapter IX, 'Upstairs and Downstairs' [provisional] (MS pages 149 to 161; in ink)

*Synopsis:* The following morning, Camilla tells Tony the full story of the missing beads — and is able to add that, in broad daylight, she has now managed to retrieve them. Tony much admires her courage in undertaking the midnight mission. He advises her, in future, to consult Winnie rather than Constance if she has serious problems and is in need of sympathetic advice. Camilla feels that Tony himself is her best advisor. After lunch, he invites her to visit his room and offers her wine, which (since they are under the Rector's roof) she cannot bring herself to drink. A slight constraint then develops.

The title, "Upstairs and Downstairs", is very lightly pencilled in *over* the chapter title, as a possibility to be borne in mind.

This short chapter was originally longer, for (as explained below) it ran without a break into what is now Chapter X. Most of the changes on the first ten pages (149 to 158) are very minor and not worth specifying, but there is an intriguing addition on page 159. Camilla has declined the glass of wine and Tony has drunk it himself without further ado. A spot of supplementary dialogue pencilled in at the bottom of the page reads "Ah, I fear I have offended you but you are very kind — you are very kind." These words are more likely to have been uttered by Camilla rather than Tony, but the notion of having giving offence is one which Camilla keeps to herself in the text as it stands and it may be that the author simply jotted down this sentence as something that might be included in a revised scenario.

At the top of page 161, after establishing that Tony was not a flirt and that the thought of commencing a romance of any kind with "his pretty slip of a foreign cousin" had probably not occurred to him, the author issued a stern command to himself: "Rewrite — end chapter with dialogue 2 or 3 sentences."

Editorial intervention means that the printed text of this chapter now ends with Camilla writing to her father "very kindly" about Tony ... and more cheerfully than before of her own prospect of a year at Essingham." In the manuscript, however, this final paragraph is followed by the one with which Chapter X now commences, namely "So matters stood for some days". The last line on page 161 is "Meanwhile she was not too proud to profit by" and the first line on page 162 continues this sentence with the words "a bit of advice of his." But a very large "R", indicating "Rewrite", is in the top left-hand corner and the heading "Chapter X" has been emphatically inserted at the top of this page. This chapter-break is very much a late-arrival and it is clear that this section of the text was theoretically destined for the melting-pot, to be replaced by something brisker. But, since the author never got round to producing this, the editor has been obliged to end Chapter IX at a slightly earlier point, where it seemed that a natural break had been reached, instead of interpreting the command about chapter divisions in too literal a sense.

Chapter X, 'In my lady's Parlour' (MS pages 162 to 172; in ink)

*Synopsis:* Camilla and Winnie become close friends. Out walking together, they are caught in the rain and take refuge at the Hall. Lady Harriet persuades Winnie to tell them more about her life in Portugal and draws her out, in particular, on the comical eccentricities and keen gambling propensities of her grandfather, the Count. Camilla is also persuaded to sing to them, with Erskine accompanying her on the piano. Winnie, throughout the afternoon, is rather quiet. The weather improves and the two girls return to the Rectory. As they walk up the drive, Camilla is greatly excited when she sees a big man with a red beard standing on the steps and throws herself into his arms with delight.

This is another very short chapter. The title, "In my lady's Parlour" (taken from the nursery rhyme, 'Goosey Goosey Gander') is inserted at the top of page 162. It clearly inspired, retrospectively, the thought that the preceding chapter might equally well be called "Upstairs and Downstairs". (In the fullness of time, the range of possibilities encompassed by such a title would also occur to others )

The text is a "fair copy" and changes are relatively few, not worth specifying.

The only point worth noting is that the author has prepared the way for the eventual appearance of a character called Ignacio, the cousin of the Count's current wife.

Hornung had momentarily forgotten (page 170) the precise title of the song in *Faust* to which he intended to refer, and left a space for the insertion of the missing word. He meanwhile added "Gonoud's" as an afterthought and the word "Jewel" has now been editorially inserted.

At the end of the chapter, the reader is as nonplussed as Winnie as to the identity of the new arrival at the Rectory. He will prove to be Camilla's father, but when we met James

Pontifex in the opening chapter he was described as "short, light-haired [and] light-eyed ... a most ordinary gentleman indeed". On his second appearance in the book, less than three weeks later, he has acquired a red beard and become "big". An explanation will be provided, in due course, as to why his physical appearance should have been altered so drastically.


## Chapter XI, untitled (MS pages 173 to 190; in pencil)

*Synopsis:* The arrival of James Pontifex for the weekend brightens up the whole household with the exception of Constance, who has to cope with the temporary mild disruptions thereby caused. He strolls round the garden with his brother, both of them in good moods and reminiscing. James is leaving for Africa without delay and expects to be away for twelve months: the Rector readily agrees to Camilla remaining under his roof during that period. On the Sunday, they all attend service at the "functional" church, where Constance plays the organ. She is in two minds about these new relatives — sympathetic one moment and hostile the next, being quick to take offence at imagined slights and jealous of the growing intimacy between Camilla and Winnie. Tony has recognised a kindred spirit from the outset and they later have a heart-to-heart talk, with James passing on some shrewd advice (reflecting experience gained from his own youthful misdemeanours) and seeking to dissuade his nephew from sewing too many wild oats. In effect, he entrusts Camilla's spiritual welfare to him. Camilla is greatly distressed by the prospect of her father's long-term absence, and wakes during the night to find him praying at the side of her bed.

The author's manuscript carries a prominent instruction to himself on the first page of this chapter, to which we will return in a moment. There are a great many deletions and insertions in the pages that follow, but nothing of any major importance. The paragraph reflecting on Constance's softer side (page 179) originally included the sentence "And Winnie had not only sharpened her sister's tongue, but had unconsciously hardened her heart against its continual cut and thrust, in her not less brusqueness of [*sic*] Camilla."

Re-reading this chapter a short time later, Hornung may well have felt dissatisfied, and even embarrassed, at the melodramatic note on which it ends. There is a touch of mawkishness here, evoking the well-known image of Little Nell on her deathbed, with her brokenhearted grandfather praying alongside. And it was, frankly, rather ridiculous that not a word — apparently — passed between father and daughter on this lachrymose occasion.

The final page of this chapter (190) was largely blank, for it contained only five lines of text. Underneath them he now jotted down, encased in two parallel balloons, some dialogue likely to have been exchanged between Camilla and her father. The first exchange runs as follows:

"The climate would have killed you"

"But you — but you?"

"Pooh! Feel my arm. — Camillasinha!"

And the second:

"It isn't too late to alter your mind —"

"Tony will be very kind to you."

"I like them all."

"Tony will be a brother to you."

"I like him too."

"And Lady Harriett Hope — "

(Quotation marks, where lacking, have been editorially inserted.) These exchanges were obviously intended to form the basis for a full-scale conversation.

Hornung then inscribed the following note in the top left-hand corner of the first page (173) of this chapter: — "<u>NB</u> Cut out all dialogues but the last 2 — add to the hist[ory] of all." One assumes that the two dialogues he had in mind were those between James Pontifex and, respectively, his nephew and his daughter.

Chapter XII (truncated), untitled (MS pages 191 to 192; in pencil)

*Synopsis:* On the Monday, Camilla conceals her depression so well that Constance decides that she is cold-hearted and indifferent to her father's departure.

The opening paragraph of this chapter, taking up slightly less than two whole pages, was all that the author managed to write. He was still making changes as he went along, however, and the third sentence originally began with the following words:

> However, those symptoms of a natural sorrow were conspicuous only by their absence; and Mr Pontifex, who, combining consolation of his niece with his one xxxxxxxx [*a heavily-deleted word equivalent to "weakness" or "pre-dilection"*], had given her a great many games of bagatelle on the Monday evening, decided that the consolation was so far unnecessary...

But the sentence (with an end still to be reached) was in danger of becoming top-heavy, so he amended and continued it as follows:

> But all such symptoms of a natural sorrow were conspicuous only by their absence; and Mr Pontifex, who had given her a great many games of bagatelle on the Monday afternoon, decided that the consolation was unnecessary; though, as she seemed fond of the game, this did not prevent him from playing with her again in the evening.

On the final page, in the penultimate sentence, Constance had prepared herself "with much genuine sympathy" for an inconsolable Camilla, but the words here given in quotation marks were deleted.

The very last words of all, although their sense is clear enough, are slightly confusing at first glance and were evidently in need of revision. The final sentence concluded (seemingly) "now she nailed down that label." Over them, Hornung wrote (seemingly) "find stronger string" [or "sting"?] but this was something that he would never get round to doing. (The editor has, rightly or otherwise, combined both sentiments in what he hopes is an appropriately-worded conclusion.)

## Fiction

It would all have started with the telegram. That, we gather, was the author's original intention. In cinematic terms, indeed, it could still work brilliantly. The first shot would be of an unknown hand passing the text of a short message across the post office counter (perhaps deleting one of the words to make it even shorter, thereby saving on expenditure). Then would come its despatch and receipt, with the standard linking shot of wires humming with activity, and then we would follow the totally untrustworthy telegraph boy as he made his dilatory way from town to village through some glorious countryside — stopping off en route to hurl stones at the local wildlife. All this time the introductory credits would be rolling. We would see the boy hand the telegram to a plumpish young lady in the Rectory garden, just as the words "Directed by A.N. Other" reached the screen, we would see her look at the envelope in mild surprise and then take it indoors to the blonde but impatient young woman supervising household arrangements. The latter would tear open the envelope, look at the message and utter a cry of astonishment. Shock, horror — "Who is this strange young woman that father is bringing here, etc?" — perhaps awakening dim recollections of *Wuthering Heights*, except that on that occasion it was a dark-haired boy (rather than a dark-haired girl). And then, with an abrupt fade-out, would come the caption "Twenty-four hours earlier", and we would find ourselves in a darkened hotel room overlooking Trafalgar Square. It is almost E.M. Forster territory (at a time slightly preceding that gentleman's official arrival on the Eng. Lit. scene), and Merchant Ivory would be in their element. And with the Pontifex family taking centre stage, it is almost Samuel Butler territory too. Clearly, Ernest William Hornung was well ahead of his time.

But on the printed page it couldn't, in the event, work out

like that. There would be too much for the Rector to summarise for the benefit of his bemused daughters and the reader needed, in any case, to be an invisible onlooker at the meeting between the two brothers, assessing for himself the characters of each of the men and the relationship between father and daughter. So the putative first chapter became the second.

Nor, sadly, could the book as a whole be brought into existence. For reasons to be explored shortly, the author came to a halt after completing eleven chapters and the opening paragraph of a twelfth. It is grossly unfair, of course, to judge the text and the plot on the basis of a narrative that it is only partially complete and one which was evidently going to be seriously revised in several places. We have no idea whether those eleven chapters represent half or even less of the book as originally conceived. But some comments on what they contain are nevertheless permissible.

The tale as we have it, developed with consummate skill and sensitivity, is a comedy of manners. In his very first published novel, *A Bride from the Bush*, Hornung had explored the comic possibilities that could result from a young Australian woman taking up residence in England. He had reversed this notion in what was probably his next (unfinished) novel, *A Graven Image*, dealing with the arrival in New South Wales of a young English woman convalescing from a long illness. Jeanette Burtrand, in that book, is staying with some relatives and so too is Camilla Pontifex, a seventeen year-old girl from Lisbon, in *Goddesses Three*. We learn what Camilla's uncle and her three English cousins think of her — and of each other — and what she, in turn, thinks of them. And then there are two "external" characters to take into account, Lady Harriett and her son Erskine. Plus the shadowy Mr Atkinson.

One longs to know what is going to happen next. But what had happened *first,* of course, was the actual title, and before

148

venturing further we should pause to wonder what factors had determined its choice. *Goddesses Three* presumably refers to Camilla, Constance and Winnie, although (with all due respect to those ladies) it is not really clear why they should have been so grandly designated. It had a fortuitous Kiplingesque ring, of course, which would have made it topical, but its derivation was really far more distant than those *Soldiers* of the same ilk.

There is nothing to suggest that Hornung was remotely interested in Greek myths. It is just conceivable, but not overwhelmingly likely, that he was familiar with William Congreve's 1710 libretto for *The Judgment of Paris: a Masque.* Its text begins with a young prince masquerading as a shepherd being rudely disturbed by Mercury, hotfoot from Jove, breathlessly warning him that Three Goddesses are heading in his direction, all contending for the prize of his golden apple. The stage-direction adds that Juno, Pallas and Venus "are seen at a distance descending in several Machines", which certainly implies that they mean business. (These were the Roman names: their Greek equivalents were Hera, Athena and Aphrodite.) And then, of course, there were a host of paintings, from Rubens and others, which depicted the Judgement in vivid detail. What Hornung is most likely to have been familiar with, however, was a popular song translated "from the French", the opening verse of which puts the situation in a nutshell:

> Goddesses three to Ida came,
> Immortal strife to settle there,
> Which was the fairest of the three,
> And which the prize of beauty should wear.

It ran to six verses and had a chorus (to be sung twice over) worded as follows:

Ev-o-e! wonderful ways
Have these goddesses now and then;
Ev-o-e! wonderful ways
For subduing the hearts of men.

(It has so far proved impossible to identify the individuals responsible for the original text and for this translation. The assumption must be that it was largely inspired by Offenbach's *La belle Hélène*, which had premiered in Paris in 1864 and in London in 1866.)

With the greatest stretch of the imagination, none of the three young women who feature in Hornung's text can be equated with any classical forbears, nor does the plot (so far as it has developed) have any points in common with the Judgement of Paris. The chorus quoted above, reflecting on the "wonderful ways" of goddesses, is the only sentiment which could be applied — and it is so trite (a statement of the obvious, it might be thought) that it is barely worth citing. Unless the fact that he had a sister called Ida is in some way significant, the mystery of why the author hit upon this title for his novel must remain unsolved: perhaps he was, indeed, simply doffing his cap to Kipling.

Returning to the truncated text, there is the distinct impression that Act One has ended, with the departure for Africa of James Pontifex, and we are left wondering just how many more Acts will follow. The action up till now has been largely confined to the Rectory and its grounds, and the smallness of the cast has conjured up a miniature world of mundane activity and unexpected tensions which would not have been altogether unfamiliar to Jane Austen.

There are clues, however, which suggest that some major events are in store and it is possible to speculate, to a limited extent, as to how things might have developed. The eleventh chapter has in many respects been a very happy one, with the two brothers reconciled and a good relationship established between James and Tony. There is an elegiac glow over the proceedings, the only discordant notes being those sounded by Constance. (And even these are muted.) The leave-taking between father and daughter may have been of a more permanent nature than either of them realised, however, and whether James is going to survive his sojourn in Mozambique is a moot point. The date on which he slips away from his childhood home (before breakfast, on all probability), after seeing it again for the first time in twenty years, and on which the Rector later endeavours to cheer up Camilla with those endless games of bagatelle, would seem to be Monday, 10 September. Tony and Erskine are scheduled to return to their respective universities in the near future and we know that Camilla is going to be at the Rectory "for months afterwards". Would Felix be accompanying his owner, one wonders, or would he be transferred to Camilla's care during Tony's absence, to serve as a keepsake and a link?

A sugar plantation is not in quite the same league as a fabulous mine belonging to a mythical king, or so it must have seemed in the mid-1890s. But even then the point may have been debatable. Given the necessary skills and determination, there was every likelihood that such a plantation could be developed into a very lucrative enterprise. In the circumstances, dirty work at the cross-roads seems almost inevitable. Our attention has been drawn to a certain gentleman called Ignacio but it is difficult to decide what sort of role he was scheduled to play in the narrative. Would he be friend or foe? We know that he is a young man (of which Erskine has taken careful note), which suggests that he might be a suitor for Camilla's hand, but we also know that the Count (perhaps unfairly) has questioned his honesty. One's sus-picion is that James is going to disappear, perhaps permanently, in the course of the proceedings, and the fact that

Ignacio has been fingered so far in advance is a cause for distinct unease.

By what God-given right, he might demand, could a dastardly Britisher, contemptuous of the peoples among whom he has lived for almost twenty years, dare to assume control of what was basically a family firm? It was surely the duty of the cousin of a third wife to rectify this deplorable state of affairs! It is not hard to envisage a scenario in which James's natural successor, Tony, ventures into foreign climes (perhaps with Erskine, in need of toughening-up, as his doughty companion) to seek justice and retribution. (The word "revenge" will never pass our hero's lips.) Scenes of derring-do and duffing-up would seem to lie ahead. Is the action going to move to Portugal (in which case we will encounter the impoverished Count and his household) or even further afield, to Mozambique itself? The only thing of which one can be reasonably sure is that the tranquility of Essingham, endowed with its timeless Roman remains and located in an unspecified part of rural England, will be left far behind for at least half-a-dozen chapters. But it will still be there, enduring as a familiar place of reassurance and stability, as the location where the main characters can be reunited in the final reel of that period-piece film.

But what will have happened to those main characters? All of them (with the possible exceptions of Winnie and Lady Harriett) are on learning-curves. The Rector has already mellowed to some extent, and it is hoped that he will even come to look with some degree of tolerance on Roman Catholics — although this cannot, of course, be guaranteed — and revise his opinion of his wayward son. The haughty Constance clearly needs taking down a peg or two and it is hoped that she will develop a greater degree of understanding so far as her Portuguese cousin is concerned. There have so far been too many misunderstandings between them, although one

152

can appreciate that Camilla's habit of shrugging her shoulders in silence has been intensely irritating and open to misconception. Camilla herself is, of course, still growing up and has much to learn, but she is adaptable and her heart is in the right place and everything will surely come right for her. Both Tony and Erskine will need to mature a little more, but they too are still relatively young and at the start of their careers; adventures overseas might well do the trick. So far as ultimate matchings-up are concerned, Tony and Camilla are surely destined for one another. But whether Erskine (in the course of coming to recognise her great qualities of sympathy, wisdom, patience and forbearance) will make do with Winnie as a consolation prize, and whether Constance will be content with Mr Atkinson as her companion for life, are matters which really lie beyond the scope of conjecture. (And substantial shadow and plump hands notwithstanding, it is not inconceivable that Lady Harriett, although old enough to be his mother, will be mischievously pursuing a private agenda and developing closer ties of her own with Mr Atkinson — who, like some of Austen's and Trollope's clergymen, may well have an eye to the main chance.)

But, exasperatingly, the book remained unfinished, and it is time to begin considering why this might have been the case.

# Fact

On 22 March 1894, at a hotel in central London, there was a joyful reunion between two brothers. The first was Ernest William Hornung, known within the family as "Willie". The second was John Peter Hornung, latterly known within the family — and thereafter to the world at large — as "Pitt". (His Portuguese wife addressed him as "Pete" and her idiosyncratic pronunciation rendered this, to the delight of all, as "Peet".)

Five years separated them, with Willie (born 1866) being the younger. There were also two other brothers, Theodore and Charles, and a third who had died when only a few months old, but the bond between these two was particularly close. It could almost be argued that Willie was destined to play Sherlock to Pitt's Mycroft, admiring his elder sibling and seeking to emulate him whenever he could — while still endeavouring to assert his individuality. He laboured mightily to overcome the twin handicaps of asthma and poor eyesight and to carve out a distinctive and equally noteworthy path for himself. In an autobiographical short story entitled 'The Jackeroo on G-Block', published in *The Strand Magazine* in April 1900, and referring to himself as 'Tahourdin', Willie tells us:

> Cursed by a distressing delicacy, and neither physically nor mentally robust, he had nevertheless an incongruous and quite unsuspected hankering after violent experiences in wild places. In part this was due to much early reading in a well-worn groove, in part to a less worthy stimulus. Tahourdin had a big brother, who had once [returned home from foreign parts] ... in romantic rags, thereafter to thrill all callers with graphic accounts of his more respectable adventures by flood and field. This had fired Tahourdin with an ignoble ambition, not so much to do and see and suffer in his turn, as to lay in a stock of yarns which should one day compare creditably with those of his brother.

Two years spent in Australia did something to even up the score, and a stream of "yarns" which followed his return home, albeit mainly of a fictional nature, did a lot more. But his brother's career had meanwhile developed by leaps and bounds and Pitt had entered a totally different league. Pitt's boyhood at the family home in Middlesbrough had been quite a wild and harum-scarum affair, with wild oats a-plenty being sown. Educated at a college in Edinburgh, he had developed a reckless taste for both women and gambling. His father (John Peter Senior) had come close to despairing of this unruly and unpredictable son. He was banished at one point to a ranch in Uruguay, but determinedly made his way home again via Lisbon — undertaking a variety of quite demeaning jobs in order to work his passage. A post was found for him in the office of a firm of local solicitors, but an affair with a cobbler's daughter led to another major confrontation with his father. While not being totally cut off without a penny, he was issued with a final ultimatum. Ordered to seek his fortunes abroad, and granted a choice of destination, he remarked (on the strength of that previous brief visit) that "Lisbon might not be a bad sort of place". His father articled him to an Austrian merchant based there and he took up residence in the Portuguese capital in 1880 or 1881.

An office-colleague with whom he became good friends was the son of a baron, the head of the Sabroso family. They lived in a disused fort, converted in a rather haphazard fashion, which stood upon a cliff overlooking the Tagus. It may just be that it was love of gambling that proved a common bond but Pitt was invited, in any case, to give up his lodgings and to move in with the family, which proved an ideal and happy arrangement. As a result of being introduced into their social circles he now came into frequent contact with the leading lights of Lisbon society. At a party in 1883 (possibly, in fact, a celebration of his own twenty-second birthday) he met a very attractive girl called Laura, with whom Pitt fell in love. They were married in April 1884, when Laura was still only sixteen. Harriett Hornung, Pitt's mother, was present at the wedding, together with one or two other members of the family (including Willie, perhaps?) and Pitt brought his bride back to England for their honeymoon. At Erdely, the family home in Middlesbrough, he introduced her to the rest of the Hornungs before whisking her off to Scotland.

Laura's father was an impoverished Count or Baron called Inácio (or Ignaçio) José de Paiva Raposo, and she had a sister called Camilla.

Ignacio (to use, henceforth, the Anglicised form of his name) had been, in his youth, extremely fond of a game of cards — and, indeed, of any other pastime which involved wagers. Gambling, one of his granddaughters (Bertha Collins) subsequently wrote, "was a vice which for years bedevilled the Portuguese upper classes. Some of these gamblers, who had already dissipated their fortunes, were prepared to stake the contents of their houses, room by room, and object by object. In one well-known house, where the painted ceilings were hanging in swags from damp and neglect, and the larder was mostly bare, the children were often sent out for meals, in twos and threes, to take pot luck with relations or friends."

But by the time Pitt first encountered him, it seems that Ignacio had become a reformed character and had renounced gambling as an active pursuit. It is not clear how large his family home was and we do not know whether Pitt moved into it or whether his wife moved out of it and joined him as part of the Sabrosos household. But, whatever the arrangement, close relations were obviously maintained with his father-in-law (roughly the same age, as it happened, as his own father, both of them being born in 1821) and sought to keep an eye on him. "Ignacio in old age [in the words of his granddaughter] was

156

absent minded to the point of eccentricity. Many were the stories in circulation about his lapses of memory. It is said that he once appeared in the presence of Royalty holding what he thought was his 'gibus' (collapsible opera hat) under his arm. Actually it was something quite different, and not nearly so smart, namely the circular wooden lid of the primitive closet of those days."

Pittt and Laura's first child, a daughter called Bertha (the granddaughter quoted above, in fact) was born in 1885. Towards the end of that year there was a crisis in the main Hornung family. The elder John Peter, a wealthy iron and coal merchant, suffered what was either a stroke or a heart attack. This had been brought about by some severe business setbacks, caused primarily by an absconding partner, and Pitt felt it his duty to hurry back to Erdely to do what he could to assist. He brought with him his wife and daughter. Here it was, in February 1886, that Laura gave birth to their son Charles. Brother Theodore, another partner in the firm, took charge of the business and eventually managed to re-establish it on a sound footing, but their father's health had been irreparably damaged. John Peter's wife, probably with Pitt in attendance, managed to bring him to London to consult a doctor who was also a personal friend, but the journey had exhausted her husband and the doctor warned that he would probably not survive the trip back to Middlesbrough. Pitt was responsible for securing a new home for them all in Waldegrave Park Road, Twickenham, not far from Strawberry Hill, and for negotiating the sale of Erdely. Unfortunately, the elder John Peter had a second seizure and died in November 1886. (Willie, who arrived back from Australia early in June 1886, apparently turned up at the former family home totally ignorant of the fact that it had changed hands.)

Laura's father died early in 1887. After the birth in July of their third child (Blanche), Pitt took his family back to

Lisbon to sort out his father-in-law's affairs and to ponder their future. (He would still be defining his profession as that of 'merchant', but the ties with his Austrian employer had now been severed.) Among other things, he took note of the fact that Ignacio had, ten years earlier, rented an estate at Mopea in central Mozambique, part of Portuguese East Africa, near the confluence of the Shire and Zambesi rivers, for the purpose of growing opium. The estate had been abandoned in 1884, following local unrest, and Pitt now wondered whether his father-in-law's scheme could be reactivated. He went off to see the estate for himself and made a valiant attempt to do just that, but an unanticipated massive flood in February 1889 wiped out (almost literally) most of the poppy-fields.

Thoroughly disheartened, Pitt now started to make his way back to Lisbon but did so via Durban. Here, providentially, he met a French sugar cane planter who convinced him that adapting the Mozambique estate for the growing of sugar cane would be the ideal way to solve the family's financial problems. Greatly excited by this notion, Pitt brought them back to Twickenham and carried out further research into the subject of sugar-growing. It seemed a sure-fire winner. By the beginning of 1890 he had managed, with the backing of friends and the Banco Lusiano, to float a company called *Companhia do Assucar de Mozambique*. In August of that year, following the birth of his second son, he took his family back to Durban and he himself journeyed on to Mopea, where the sugar plantation would prove to be a massively profitable enterprise: the first canes were cut in the summer of 1893. (The rest is history, and goes far beyond the scope of this present exercise: suffice to say that Pitt eventually became a millionaire.)

By March 1894, therefore, Pitt had been absent from England for a period of three and a half years. Willie, in the meantime, had in September 1893 married Constance Doyle, the sister of the novelist. Returning to their Chelsea flat on 21

March from a hugely enjoyable short holiday in Davos, with Conan Doyle and his wife, they were delighted to find a note from Pitt announcing that he was back in London. The following morning Willie rushed round to his bedroom at the First Avenue Hotel in High Holborn, an establishment then regarded as the last word in luxury, and caught up on the latest developments. They dined at the hotel that evening, accompanied by their respective wives (who got on famously), and next day Pitt and Laura were guests of honour at the Chelsea flat. Willie was pleased to note that his brother would not be returning to Africa until the second half of April, which meant that he would be in England for the best part of a month. (It is possible that Constance was already slightly acquainted with Pitt and Laura, since —like two of her sisters — she had recently been employed as a governess in Lisbon.)

Constance, it should be mentioned at this point, was an extremely good-looking young woman ("perfectly lovely" was one admirer's description) and there had been at least a couple of rival suitors before Willie appeared on the scene in 1892. Jerome K. Jerome recalled "a handsome girl" with curly hair and a fresh complexion who "might have posed as Brunhilda": he found her cheerful and lively, with a sympathetic nature. The mention of Brunhilda conjures up an image of a statuesque Wagnerian heroine and it has to be acknowledged that George Gissing, while finding her robust, healthy and good-humoured, "with wonderfully bright eyes", was somebody else who considered her rather large. (In a family group photograph, she appears to be dark-haired and shorter than Willie: but the suspicion must be that Willie, in the back row alongside Conan Doyle, was standing on something.) She was a staunch Roman Catholic, a faith to which she adhered (unlike her brother and, perhaps, her husband) until her dying day.

Both Willie and Pitt were happily married, therefore, and so too (since the summer of 1892) was their brother Charles. But their fourth brother, Theodore, had been a widower since 1888 and had shouldered the responsibility of bringing up two young daughters (now aged fourteen and nine). Some good news, on the other hand, was that their sister Ida, three years older than Pitt, had married a clergyman.

Ida's wedding had taken place almost two years earlier, in April 1892, and Willie had particular cause to remember the event because (for reasons unknown) he had seriously cut his hand at some point in the proceedings and had been physically unable to write for a good many weeks. Such a mishap was a major setback for someone solely dependent on income from his novels and short stories. Having left the Waldegrave household in 1891 to take rooms in central London, he was unable to cope by himself and was obliged to return to the family circle for a time. His health in general deteriorated and he had several attacks of asthma. He was frequently awake for half the night. His publishers, in the meantime, were pressing him for a novel he had undertaken to supply. Urgent assistance was required, and to his rescue there came *another* lady whose name also happened to be Constance.

The lady in question was Constance McNally. She was twelve years older than Willie and the daughter of a bootmaker living in Peckham. Beginning her working life as a dress-maker's assistant, by 1891 she had become a fully qualified "short hand and type writer" and was clearly skilled in her profession. The means whereby links were established between her and the Waldegrave household are unknown. (Is there any remote possibility, one wonders, that she could have been that cobbler's daughter with whom young Pitt had once been involved?) She proved, at any rate, a tower of strength at Willie's time of need, taking down dictation from him at all hours of the day and night over a period of ten weeks. It was thanks to her assistance that he was able to deliver to his publishers a novel called *Tiny Luttrell*, which came out in April

1893, and she also assisted him with the opening stages of a novella called *The Unbidden Guest*. But by September 1892, when Willie was fit enough to play cricket, their initial working relationship had come to an end. (Constance, who never married and lived in Peckham for most of her long life, would assist him again in the 1900s — and by 1911, it is interesting to note, she would be working as a shorthand typist for "sugar planter manufacturers".)

At which point, it is time to look again at the truncated text of *Goddesses Three* and to draw certain conclusions.

# Conclusions

Willie Hornung in 1894 was becoming steadily well-known in literary circles but had not quite reached the pinnacle of his profession. While prominent among the second-rankers, the high ground occupied by the current giants such as Henry James, Thomas Hardy and (most recently) Rudyard Kipling was still some way beyond his attainment. (It was not even clear that his brother-in-law, Conan Doyle, had yet been accepted as a fully-fledged member of that exalted circle.)

Hornung was a full-time writer of short stories and novels, most of them either set directly in Australia or else with strong Australian connections. It was the only profession he knew, and he was solely dependent upon the success of his output for a steady income with which to support himself and his household. He was always in need of raw material from which to hone fresh fiction. While still learning on the job, he was almost certainly convinced that (potentially, at any rate) he was capable of greater things and that he was gradually developing the alchemist's ability to transmute lead into gold. Everything was grist to his mill and he needed to be alive to the possibilities of any real-life situation which could serve as the basis for a new story. There was an element of practicality, but also ruthlessness, in this approach.

It will be recalled that the first canes at Mopea had been cut in the summer of 1893, and news of this great event would have been transmitted to England without delay. It is surmised that in the winter of 1893/94, pondering on what would be a good subject for his next book, it occurred to Willie that the fresh trail blazed by his brother was presenting him, in effect, with a ready-made scenario. The Mozambique enterprise was an exciting one, and could serve as the foundation-stone for a novel in which (just for once!) there would be no reference whatsoever to Australia. The edifice to be erected would be, of

162

course, primarily fictitious, but it would provide him with the scope for developments on a number of fronts. As noted earlier, Willie had become adept at exploring, with sensitivity, the comic potential of a young heroine abruptly deposited in a foreign land, with misunderstandings and confusions on both sides to be sorted out. But he was also becoming skilled at plotting adventure and mystery stories, with a satisfying element of suspense and a few surprises and twists before the final denouement. Here was an opportunity for the two fields in which he specialised to be combined — and, in consequence, it might even prove a best-seller. All the ingredients for a first-rate story, located in the present, were, seemingly, to hand. And so he set to work.

There is no knowing how far he had got in his narrative before the holiday at Davos (to which he had been summoned by Conan Doyle) intervened. He would have been aware, however, that a jubilant Pitt and his wife intended to return to England for a short break in the near future and that there would probably be a re-union in a London hotel room. This was the location chosen, therefore, for the meeting between the two Pontifex brothers. We are duly introduced to James, who is described as "short, light-haired [and] light-eyed ... a most ordinary gentleman indeed". This must surely be a description of Pitt, as Willie remembered him from August 1890. When the two brothers did actually meet again, however, Willie was startled to find that Pitt now looked totally different. He had put on a substantial amount of weight (and his previously modest beard may have become bushier since their last encounter). Willie's mental image of his elder brother would henceforth be radically different from the previous one. This alteration was duly reflected in the text of *Goddesses Three*, when, on being re-introduced into the narrative after an absence of less than three weeks, James Pontifex has acquired a red beard and become "big". (Revisions to that description of him in the opening chapter would obviously have been required.)


To say that the Pontifex family is a mirror-image of the Hornung family would be an exaggeration, but not a gross one.

The most obvious demonstration of this is, of course, the fact that the career of James Pontifex follows that of Pitt Hornung, almost undeviatingly. Like James, Pitt had married a beautiful young Portuguese girl — and her father, in both instances, was an impoverished and eccentric Count. And, just as Pitt had been in 1890, so James in 1894 is actively involved in floating a company to exploit the potential of a sugar plantation in Mozambique, seeking support from a range of backers.

James's young wife had died young, but we gather that Camilla is a replica of her mother and it is clear that her character was based upon that of Laura de Paiva Raposo, Pitt's wife and Willie's sister-in-law. (And Laura had a sister called Camilla, who may have resembled her in many respects.) But Laura's husband *also* served as the inspiration for two separate roles, and to a much greater extent. For we are told that Tony is behaving in much the same manner as James had behaved at the same age. There are only occasional, albeit tantalising, references to the earlier life of James, but we do know that both Pitt and Tony, as they entered into young manhood, had developed a keen interest in the opposite sex and a relish for gambling. Tony, in short, embodies the young version of Pitt, while James is the older, wiser version, in a position to dispense advice.

A third real-life character, although it is only at one stage removed that we have so far encountered him, would appear to have been (at first sight) the aforementioned impoverished and eccentric Portuguese Count. One strongly suspects that the tales which Camilla told first Tony and then the Hopes were, word for word, the tales which Laura told her husband's family — but with one very crucial distinction, for she would have been talking about not just one Count but *two*. The first would indeed have been her father, Count Ignacio de Paiva Raposo, but the second would have been Count Simao (?) Sabroso, whose family had been so accommodating so far as Pitt was concerned. It was the Sabroso Count who lived in the fort overlooking the Tagus and who gambled so wildly. (Ignacio had indeed been a gambler in his youth but had apparently succeeded in curing himself of the addiction.) What Willie did, therefore, was to merge the two personalities into one.

Thereafter the parallels between the two families, while present, are rather more diffused.

Pitt's wayward behaviour as a young man had been the despair of his father. Patience had been tried to the uttermost. Voices had been raised and ultimatums had been issued — he had been banished from the family circle, not once but twice, until such time as he could demonstrate that he was capable of behaving in a responsible fashion. The Rector, similarly, is in a state of almost perpetual despair over the reckless behaviour of Tony, who (to his eyes) is going rapidly to the dogs. It is quite possible that some of his outbursts, on this particular subject, echoed those of John Peter Hornung Senior. But this is not so suggest that the Rector is remotely similar, in other respects, to the author's father, who was apparently a genial, cheerful individual.

The Rector was, like Theodore Hornung, a widower with two daughters to bring up and it is conceivable (without knowing too much about him) that Theodore did serve as a model for the reverent gentleman.

And what are we to make of Constance Pontifex? One is initially startled to find that an attractive lady bearing that particular Christian name features in the book, for the thought springs to mind that this must surely be a representation of Hornung's own wife, in which case he would be skating on very thin ice indeed. For the fictional Constance, albeit capable and resourceful when it came to running the household, is undeniably of a bossy disposition and takes after her father in being dogmatic, narrow-minded and intolerant and sweeping in her judgments, especially where Catholics are concerned. She would seem to be precisely the opposite of the real-life Constance Hornung, who (while bearing a resemblance to Brunhilda) was good-humoured and cheerful — and also a devoted Catholic. It is just conceivable that Willie was thinking of Constance McNally, of whose appearance we have no knowledge, who was also capable and resourceful, but far more likely that he had conferred the name upon the elder Miss Pontifex in a purely playful mood — just as the Christian name of the author's mother (a widow) had been bestowed on Lady Harriett Hope (another widow). It should perhaps be borne in mind that a relationship is, after a fashion, developing between Constance and a clergyman and that Ida Hornung, the author's sister, had married a clergyman two years earlier.

James Pontifex and John Peter Hornung the Younger (i.e., Pitt) have different Christian names but the names of James and John, the sons of Zebedee, have been yoked together for two thousand years and come very close to being interchangeable. (A certain Dr Watson happily answers to both of them.)

As noted already, Camilla was the name of Laura's sister and Ignacio was the name of her father.

The text as we have it starts with James's arrival on 22 August and ends with his departure on 10 September, a period amounting to almost three weeks — roughly equivalent to the length of time that Pitt's visit to England had lasted.

The manner in which the book may have been intended to develop has been examined already. The one remaining mystery, however, is why it should suddenly have come to a halt. It is possible that some of the action was intended to take place abroad, in which case Willie would have needed to see Lisbon for himself, if he had not done so already, in order to thoroughly familiarise himself with the character of that city and perhaps acquire a better knowledge of the Portuguese language. He might even have contemplated venturing so far afield as the African jungle in search of authentic experience. In the opinion of the current editor, however, Willie reached the conclusion that it was really out of the question for him to base a work of fiction so blatantly on the career of his elder brother. Pitt and his achievements were gradually becoming well-known and some of the sentiments emanating from the mouth of James Pontifex, especially on the shortcomings of the Portuguese people ("kind-hearted ... [but so] hopeless"), might well have proved acutely embarrassing to him. It would seem, moreover. that Tahourdin was seeking to take a free ride to fame and fortune by clinging to the coat-tails of his big brother rather than pioneering a distinct path of his own.

Perhaps, in the search for that path, there might be more to be said for fashioning a story about someone called Deedes *major*, a debonair ex-public school chappie down on his luck, who (banished to Australia) craftily robs a bank. 'After the Fact', a tale written in 1895, would serve as trail-blazer for the adventures of the most celebrated gentleman-thief ever created. But that person's life would be very much another story, located in a totally different world from the gentility of Essingham, and in the last analysis rather unsavoury — although tender-hearted Winnie would doubtless have discovered some redeeming traits in the miscreant. (For, she might have argued, somebody who had been a Cambridge man, just as Tony was, or played cricket, just as Erskine did, could by no stretch of the imagination be dismissed as wholly bad, or beyond the reach of redemption.

167

The manuscript of *Goddesses Three* was meanwhile tucked away in a dark corner, with scarcely a soul being aware of its existence, and one hundred and ten years would go by before it finally emerged into the public domain. Another ten would then elapse before it was examined in detail. This is the first time that it has appeared in print. Catalogued as MS 127/A/2/1/5, it is housed in the splendid Cadbury Research Library of the University of Birmingham. I must acknowledge, with gratitude, my indebtedness to the Librarian and her colleagues for granting me access to it and for the subsequent provision of a photocopy, which (with the aid of a Sherlockian magnifying glass) has been mulled over for many hours. I am also indebted to Dick Sveum and Tim Johnson of the University of Minnesota at Minneapolis (owner and custodian respectively) for very kindly supplying me, in addition to many other things, with a copy of the letter which Willie wrote to Conan Doyle on 22 March 1894, describing the long-awaited reunion with his brother Pitt earlier that day.

I must once again acknowledge the very great assistance of Mr Bernard Hornung, on behalf of the Hornung family, for sanctioning its publication, for answering a good many questions about the career of Pitt, his great-great-grandfather, and, not least, for passing on to me his late father's copy of *J.P. Hornung: a family portrait* by B.M. Collin (1970), which has proved an invaluable source of information. Finally, I must thank my friend Maureen Hubbard ('Mo') for checking over, with eagle-eyed enthusiasm, the typed text of *Goddesses Three* and for detecting a batch of small errors which had escaped the editor's own scrutiny. But for any remaining errors in this little study he is, of course, solely responsible.

Peter Rowland
Wanstead, London
January 2017

#0138 - 230117 - C0 - 210/148/9 - PB - DID1730306